# SUPERNATURAL

# SUPERNATURAL

*Writings on an Unknown History*

# RICHARD SMOLEY

JEREMY P. TARCHER | PENGUIN
*a member of Penguin Group (USA) Inc.*
*New York*

JEREMY P. TARCHER/PENGUIN
Published by the Penguin Group
Penguin Group (USA) Inc., 375 Hudson Street, New York, New York 10014, USA • Penguin
Group (Canada), 90 Eglinton Avenue East, Suite 700, Toronto, Ontario M4P 2Y3, Canada
(a division of Pearson Penguin Canada Inc.) • Penguin Books Ltd, 80 Strand, London WC2R 0RL,
England • Penguin Ireland, 25 St Stephen's Green, Dublin 2, Ireland (a division of
Penguin Books Ltd) • Penguin Group (Australia), 707 Collins Street, Melbourne, Victoria 3008,
Australia (a division of Pearson Australia Group Pty Ltd) • Penguin Books India Pvt Ltd,
11 Community Centre, Panchsheel Park, New Delhi–110 017, India • Penguin Group (NZ),
67 Apollo Drive, Rosedale, Auckland 0632, New Zealand (a division of Pearson
New Zealand Ltd) • Penguin Books (South Africa), Rosebank Office Park, 181 Jan Smuts Avenue,
Parktown North 2193, South Africa • Penguin China, B7 Jiaming Center,
27 East Third Ring Road North,Chaoyang District, Beijing 100020, China

Penguin Books Ltd, Registered Offices: 80 Strand, London WC2R 0RL, England

Most Tarcher/Penguin books are available at special quantity discounts for bulk purchase for sales
promotions, premiums, fund-raising, and educational needs. Special books or book excerpts also can
be created to fit specific needs. For details, write Penguin Group (USA) Inc. Special Markets,
375 Hudson Street, New York, NY 10014.

Library of Congress Cataloging-in-Publication Data

Smoley, Richard, date.
Supernatural : writings on an unknown history / Richard Smoley.
p.      cm.
Includes bibliographical references and index.
ISBN 978-0-399-16182-7
1. Occultism.   2. Parapsychology.   3. Supernatural—History.   4. Supernatural (Theology)
5. Prophecies (Occultism)   I. Title.
BF1411.S667    2013                    2012039947
130—dc23

Printed in the United States of America
1   3   5   7   9   10   8   6   4   2

*Book design by Gretchen Achilles*

While the author has made every effort to provide accurate telephone numbers, Internet addresses,
and other contact information at the time of publication, neither the publisher nor the author assumes
any responsibility for errors, or for changes that occur after publication. Further, the publisher does
not have any control over and does not assume any responsibility for author or third-party websites or
their content.

FOR WILLIAM ST. JOHN SMOLEY

# ACKNOWLEDGMENTS

While I certainly feel that I owe a debt of gratitude to the large number of people, past and present, who have given me inspiration and insights about the subjects discussed here, there are some who deserve special mention. First and foremost is David Jones, editor of *New Dawn* magazine in Australia, who originally solicited many of the articles that appear in this collection. Most of these pieces, in fact, first appeared in *New Dawn*: "An Encounter with the Ancient Wisdom," "Does Prophecy Work?," "Secrets of *The Da Vinci Code*," "2012," "René Guénon and the Kali Yuga," "Atlantis Then and Now," "Hidden Masters," "The Science of Thought," "The Mysterious *Kybalion*," "Demons Among Us," and "Toxic Prayer." An earlier version of "Masonic Civilization" was first published in *Gnosis: A Journal of the Western Inner Traditions*. "*A Course in Miracles* Revisited" and "Cultivating the Field of Images" were first published in *Parabola*, while "The Dual Nature of Reality" first appeared in *Quest: Journal of the Theosophical Society in America*.

Thanks are also due to Mitch Horowitz, editor-in-chief at Tarcher/Penguin, who has provided encouragement and support for my work for many years now, and who is responsible for the final shape of this collection, as well as its title. I am very grateful to him for all his help.

Finally, I would like to thank my dear wife, Nicole, for her care and support, and my two little sons, Robert and William, for the loving family that they have helped create.

# CONTENTS

# PREFACE

CENTURIES DON'T ALWAYS END WHEN the calendar says they should. Historians speak of the "long nineteenth century," which stretched from 1789 (the start of the French Revolution) to 1914 (the outbreak of World War I). Some also speak of the "short twentieth century," from 1914 to the end of the Cold War in 1990. If this is so, it seems to me that we now sit in an interregnum, when the twentieth century has ended but the twenty-first has not yet begun. The age we live in is a waiting room.

The essays in this collection span fifteen years of this period, from 1997 to 2012. While they say little about topical issues, as I look back on them I see that they reflect the mood of that unsettled time. In the last quarter of the twentieth century, people had intermittently allowed themselves to hope for a massive awakening of society, but the first decade of the new millennium seemed to shoot down these hopes. Instead many great institutions stiffened and contracted, giving license to the worst aspects of human character—particularly greed—and behaving as if the better angels of our nature did not exist.

Whatever these facts may mean for history and politics, they also suggest that the moral and intellectual framework of civilization has weakened. The two worldviews governing the mind of the West—Christianity and scientific materialism—have begun to curl and shrink and blacken like scraps of paper in a fire. During the previous two centuries, the old Christian cosmology collapsed in the face of scientific discovery. The tidy biblical universe that was only six thousand years old was found to be too small to contain the enormous upheavals that were found in the geological and biological records. Even worse, Christianity was tried and found wanting in terms of its own standards. The churches were shown not only to have consistently violated the teachings of their founder but often to have embodied these violations in their own institutions. Persecution, bigotry, and intolerance can be expected to crop up in any organization, but what are we to say when these offenses have become part of the stuff of which that organization is made?

In recent years scientific materialists have gloried in these disclosures. But closer investigation does not give any reason for great confidence in materialism either. Its critique of Christianity has frequently consisted of a kind of enormous *ad hominem* argument—pointing at the shortcomings of the institutions in order to show the weakness of the faith. But this has not invalidated the ethos of Christianity; it has only shown that people frequently fail to live up to it. The proselytizers for materialism have tried—with imperfect success—to prove that we don't need Christianity in order to embrace the moral ideals of Christianity, but they have not produced any ethical system that is better. Indeed much of moral philosophy in the past hundred years has consisted of taking Christian ethics and trying to justify them through purely rational considerations, such as the doctrine of the greatest good for the greatest number. But these attempts have never managed to uplift or inspire anyone outside of a tiny circle of intellectuals.

Furthermore, science may have invalidated the literal meaning of Genesis, but scientific claims about the origin and nature of the universe are showing their own weaknesses. Some still treat Einstein's relativity and quantum physics as startling new discoveries, but these discoveries are now around a hundred years old. More recent theories—such as superstring theory and the existence of countless other universes—are intriguing, but their proponents often sound like the astronomers of the late period of the Ptolemaic theory of the solar system, who had to multiply the number of epicycles in the planets' orbits in order to account for increasing inconsistencies in the data. There has long been talk of new paradigms in science, but many of the current paradigms are starting to look old. And they remain as far from answering the existential questions about the purpose and nature of our own being as they have ever been.

I believe there are ways out of these impasses, and I've suggested steps in this direction in my previous books, such as *The Dice Game of Shiva*, in which I tried to show that consciousness is not a mere side effect of neural processes but is integral to the workings of the universe at all levels. For obvious reasons I won't try to recapitulate those arguments here. In this book I want to illustrate a different perspective that casts light on many current spiritual issues, ranging from prophecy to the reality of psychic phenomena to the existence of angels and devils. For those who are familiar with my previous books, I hope this one will provide some illuminating sidelights on vital issues that I did not cover there; new readers, I hope, will find this a bracing introduction to my work.

The perspective I'm presenting is not, strictly speaking, unknown, although it may be so for many because it has been long buried in the underbrush of cultural discourse. I'm speaking of the perspective of the esoteric traditions, which have never entirely vanished throughout the course of Western civilization, although they have often had to go underground. One of the central features of esotericism is revealed in its name, which comes from the Greek *esoterikos*, derived from roots meaning "further in." In one sense this requires going further into the hidden teachings that underlie all the great religions of the world, but it also asks us to go deeper into ourselves. In this way we can move toward answers to questions that constantly come up among people today regarding such things as prophecy, psychic phenomena, and alternate realities.

For many people, these questions are genuinely pressing. They arise not out of intellectual musings but out of experiences that go against the grain of ordinary opinion and belief. It's not always possible to give definitive answers, but I believe it is possible to give answers that are better than the ones that conventional science and religion usually offer.

To deal more specifically with the content of these essays, I would say that I'm attempting to see patterns of truth in some of the questions that come up around mystical or occult subjects: what is the myth of Atlantis about? Can prayer hurt as well as heal? Can prophecy tell us about the future? How do our thoughts affect reality? Do demons exist? As these essays show, I believe these questions have to be taken seriously in the light of the whole range of human experience. We don't need to reject paranormal experiences en masse to convince ourselves that we're rational and skeptical people, but we do need to investigate them critically and insightfully.

Underlying all these essays is woven a theme that, I believe, is the most important and sublime in all religious literature. It is the concept of the true "I," the Self that exists within and behind each of our individual personalities. It can stand back from any and all of our own experiences, the most intimate and the most painful, and regard them impartially, objectively, and compassionately. It is toward this "I" that the great spiritual traditions of the world all point, each of them of course using different names. Having some direct experience of it, however short and fleeting, enlightens the entire being, and the dull weight of the nerves and fibers of the body light up like a tree on fire. For some, this experience is transitory; for others, apparently permanent. But I don't believe that anyone can experience this awakening without being transformed by it forever. It is to point toward this awakening that this book is ultimately aimed.

WHEATON, ILLINOIS

*February 2012*

*One*

# AN ENCOUNTER
# WITH THE
# ANCIENT WISDOM

We're going down to London to see a friend of mine. Want to come?" The speaker—Dave, an odd-looking man with a scraggly beard and extremely thick glasses—was a member of the Kabbalah group at Oxford to which I went faithfully every Wednesday evening. The year was 1978 or early '79.

I wasn't particularly eager to take the trip, but in the interest of broadening my horizons, I decided I would. And so that Saturday five of us piled precariously into Dave's three-wheeled motorcycle, of the color the French call *caca d'oie*, and made the hour's drive from Oxford to London.

It was a day that burned itself into my mind for several reasons. To begin with, there was something quintessentially English about the experience. Our first stop was a large and seedy pub somewhere in northwest

London—complete with all the stereotypical trimmings: etched-glass windows, dark furniture, the hazy smell of stale beer and tobacco, and even a drunken old man singing "It's a Long Way to Tipperary" to himself at full volume. Unwisely, I found myself drinking three pints of Guinness and cider in quick succession. Not an ideal preparation for an encounter that the *I Ching* calls "meeting with the great man," but then I was unaware that I was about to have such an encounter.

Our motley assemblage proceeded to the neighborhood of Maida Vale, where we parked on a street lined with three-story brick buildings of flats and marched up to the top floor of one of them. When we were admitted, we went down the hall of a long, narrow flat and entered the kitchen, a room that I will always remember as both remarkably dingy and remarkably magical. The walls were a lifeless green, and the air was heavy with the smoke of roll-your-own cigarettes. A large image of the Kabbalistic Tree of Life, with Tarot cards affixed to the tree's paths, was painted on the near wall, half-hidden by a cluttered kitchen table. Seated in the corner, wearing a dark and not terribly clean sweater and producing the smoke that pervaded the room, was a man I shall never forget.

Although seated—he did not get up to greet us—it was clear that he was short and stocky. He had longish dark hair and a beard, black-rimmed glasses, and a broad face, kindly and shrewd to equal degrees, that somewhat resembled portrait busts of Socrates. There was an air of impish wisdom about him that years later would lead me to wonder half-seriously, when I saw *The Empire Strikes Back*, whether the character Yoda was not a cruel but very witty caricature of Glyn.

He was not, of course, rooted to that old armchair in the corner of his kitchen—over the years I would see him in any number of settings—but it was as if he were, as if he were a fixed and stable point around which the ever-changing world revolved. What he said to us all that afternoon is hopelessly lost in the back chambers of my memory. The Guinness-and-ciders did their work, and I nodded off occasionally. If it was an inauspicious introduction to ancient wisdom in the modern world, it nevertheless left an indelible mark on me.

Glyn—though it no doubt would have irked him to hear me say it—was the closest thing to a Master that I have ever met. In the nearly three decades in which I knew him, I did not see him often—there would be five- or six-year stretches after my return to America when I had no contact with him—but I would make a point of seeing him whenever I went to England up to the time of his death in 2007. More than once I went for that purpose alone.

What did I learn? Some of the words I heard were familiar right away—the Kabbalah, the Tree of Life,

Buddhism—while others—Gurdjieff, Ouspensky, Sufism—aroused only the dimmest associations in me. Even apart from this, when I try to summarize the knowledge I gained in terms of intellectual discourse, my resources cave in. I find that the first thing I come up with is what I can fumblingly call a sense of *scale*.

It has happened to me more than occasionally. I remember encountering it when I was a small child, sitting at parties of my parents'. Usually I was unimaginably bored by the subjects the adults talked about, but sometimes the discussion would turn to the paranormal—Atlantis, UFOs, Edgar Cayce, and other matters that were of great interest to my father. No one knew very much about these things, but quite apart from the content of what was said, I noticed that the mood changed. Suddenly we were no longer confined, or quite so confined, in a small living room, but the horizons of the universe seemed to open up subtly and we were surrounded by a vast and limitless space that was both awe-inspiring and somewhat terrifying. I would later have the same experience in my Kabbalah group in Oxford, at Glyn's, and in other places and groups in which I studied. Although I was aware of this dimension as a child, it was only half-consciously. It would take much longer to bring this awareness into focus.

Hence to speak purely personally, the first lesson I learned in my encounter with the ancient wisdom was precisely this sense of scale—the recognition that earthly reality and the mundane quibblings of our daily existence are not the only, or even the most important, reality. And the more I have seen of the ancient wisdom traditions that have come down to our time, the more I believe that this lesson is fundamental to them.

Glyn's background was in the Western magical tradition. As the painting on his kitchen wall suggested, he used the Kabbalah and the Tarot as a spiritual vocabulary, and I would later learn that he had his own connection with what is sometimes called the Old Religion—the native British mystery tradition that is said to have preceded Christianity and even the coming of the Celts, the religion that may have inspired the builders of Stonehenge and Avebury, and which is still undoubtedly alive in England to this day. But there was no sectarianism in what Glyn taught; he moved easily between the mysteries of the Hebrew letters, the epistles of Paul, and the half-forgotten native faith of the ancient British.

I have said that one of the first things I learned from this version of the ancient wisdom was this sense of scale, but I don't believe that this experience was unique to me. On the contrary, I sense that most, perhaps all, people have it at some point, whether it is aroused by a visit to some sacred spot, a magnificent natural vista, or the panoply of the night sky. And yet for nearly everyone, this experience is inadvertent. It comes and goes as it wills, and usually leaves behind nothing more than a faint memory to haunt the imagination. And the ancient wisdom is about more than transitory moments of awe; it is about making some conscious connection with the source of that awe.

Hence meditation. Countless books have been written about meditation, and countless more are continuing to be written. Some very competently set out techniques; others spell out the benefits to health and well-being; still others advocate the practice as a means of reaching supreme illumination (although the number of people who have actually reached that illumination appears to be shockingly small). But I have seen very few that speak to the deepest and most genuine power that lies behind meditation, which Glyn pointed out to me.

Glyn had a restless and inventive mind. Not only did he understand many mystical systems, but created systems of his own as indefatigably as a hobbyist in his workshop turns out bookshelves and stools. In his later years, he developed an interest in what he called the "peasant tradition of Europe"—a relative of the ancient religion of the British Isles that, in his own way, he was perpetuating. At one point he told me about the Carbonari, the old guild of Italy and France that made a profession of charring wood until it turned to charcoal. And it is the case, as more than one source has pointed out, that the guilds of

Europe—known in France as the *compagnonnages*—have retained much of the wisdom of the initiates. But even so, what esoteric significance could one possibly find in this humblest of practices? For Glyn, it was a symbol of meditation—which is, he said, "reducing the mind to its simplest essence." Just as wood is burned down to produce charcoal—carbon—so the process of meditation refines the mind so that it attains its simplest and most absolute form.

I have practiced meditation, both in the form that Glyn taught me and in others, for some thirty-three years now, and again I am stymied when it comes to spelling out the concrete results. I have no way of knowing how it has affected my heart rate or my blood pressure, or whether it makes me more peaceful and serene; but then I have been doing it for so long that I no longer know what I would be without it. Instead, as I grope toward an answer to the question of what meditation does, I return yet again to that sense of scale that I have already mentioned. Meditation does not necessarily produce that sense in each session, but, I would say, it does manage to make some connection between that sense of scale in the outside world and a similar sense that you can find within yourself. It leads to the intuition that your own depths and the depths of the universe are one and the same.

Given all this, how can you make a connection between this vast world within and mundane reality? How can you

avoid the danger of spiritual narcissism, whereby you become so fascinated by the inner world that the outer world
no longer holds out interest? Part of Glyn's answer to this
question lay in *observation*. As the twentieth-century spiritual teacher G. I. Gurdjieff pointed out, we pass our daily
lives in a kind of waking trance. We walk down the street
barely seeing what is before our eyes, enraptured by a
sometimes pleasing, sometimes frightening, sometimes
boring sequence of thoughts, images, and emotions that
swallow up our attention. We perceive many things but
observe very few. If there is to be some connection between
the inner and the outer world, it has to be through a conscious effort at awareness. While Gurdjieff taught self-
remembering and self-observation, there is a correlated
practice that takes this approach one step further. Glyn
called it "wide attention."

His own powers of observation were remarkable. At
one point I was in a residential course that had been set up
under his auspices, but which he did not, for the most part,
attend. This course was on some country property. At one
point a friend of mine took me aside and said, "Don't tell
anyone, but there's a tree over there that has some
plums that are just about ripe." It was our little secret
(although I gathered that it was one that had circulated
with considerable freedom among the participants). At a
certain point Glyn turned up to teach a class. He sat him-

self down on an ottoman in the large room that served as a classroom, looked out the window, saw the tree, and said, "Plums! Got to get me some of those before I go." He zeroed in at once on an item of interest that I had totally failed to notice until someone told me about it.

Essentially, wide observation is nothing more than expanding the scope of your senses to take in the fullness of the setting, whether this is the view out of a window of a country house or a cluttered little office. Say you are in a room. Normally we are only aware of two or three items in our view—perhaps fewer than that. But what if your consciousness expanded to fill the entire scene of your experience at any given time? Again, we all have this capacity to a degree. It is why practically everyone can sense the atmosphere of a place, whether it imparts a serene calm or a gut-wrenching dread. But we are usually aware of such things only in acute circumstances, and we neglect this capacity when we are in more neutral settings.

One way of developing this sense of "wide attention" would be to sense the four corners of the room you are in, not only with your sight, but with a kind of sense of touch that is able, with a little training, to extend itself outward and fill a space. You can take this sense of observation further to include the view from the windows outside, and the smells and sounds in the vicinity. This is "wide attention."

If you maintain this awareness of the room's corners—
say by imagining a column of light in each one—you cannot only expand your own consciousness but change the
room's atmosphere. While most people affect their envi-
rons in this way to some degree, it is usually only uncon-
sciously and haphazardly. Great sages seem to have this
capacity under conscious control. They can change the
mood of a room simply by an act of will. Other, more
saintly types exude a sense of peace and well-being from
themselves at all times. They have made such contact with
their own depths that beneficent forces flow from them
more or less automatically. But that is an advanced stage.

All of which raises the issue of power. And by "power"
I mean something fairly specific. It may be best described
by an example. Charles R. Tetworth, who also works within
the native British magical tradition, writes:

> The most effective magic that I have observed was
> performed by a group of people who were sitting
> around in an ordinary room, in an odd assortment
> of chairs, wearing ordinary clothes and chattering
> as usual. Then they just stopped smoking, drinking
> tea, and chatting. The leader reminded them why
> they were there, checked the roles each was to fulfill
> and then, without apparent evocation or invocation,
> proceeded with the matter. To me, as an observer,

the atmosphere in the room became electric. It felt as though danger was present. In the course of time, I happened to attend a seminar on a comparatively abstruse branch of morphology and—whether or not this was a coincidence—one of the speakers talked about the very matter that the magical group had attempted to bring into consciousness.

Another British magus, Aleister Crowley, defined magic as "the Science and Art of causing Change to occur in conformity with will." One could add that this "Science and Art" involves the use of power—the "electric" atmosphere in the room during the ritual that was so powerful as to possess a sense of danger.

From even this short discussion it should be obvious that power and attention are closely related. Perhaps at some level they are identical. In any event, power is, under ordinary circumstances, fairly diffuse. It is only when the will and the attention have been trained that it can be directed in the intense, "electric" way that a magical ritual requires.

Training this attention can take a number of forms. With meditation and observation, we have already seen two of these forms. But there is another way that one can become proficient in the use of power and attention. It is through craft.

Probably everyone has some experience of the fact that manufactured objects differ in the kinds of aura that they possess. Something produced industrially—say, an ordinary pair of plastic flip-flops or a cheap toy—ordinarily has very little. Occasionally one encounters some things, usually made partly by hand, that have more of an aura—such as a pair of extremely well-made shoes or a fine piece of blown glass. This is not coincidental. Industrial manufacture requires very little attention on any one individual item; the thing passes through an assembly line and that is all. Objects that require handwork to some degree have received more of that subtle force known as "attention." A superior craftsman can put so much attention into his work that even homely things such as a coffee table can possess an aura of their own. When this kind of achievement is taken to a maximal degree, the result is known as great art.

Not everyone is going to be a great artist or even a skilled craftsman. But there are ways in which this form of attention can be cultivated in the making of objects. For this reason ritual magicians are often given the task of making their own implements. Of course something as good or better can be bought in a store; in the United States, there are plenty of shops where you can buy not only crystals and New Age jewelry but wands and cups for magical rituals, many of them handsomely executed. But even in these cases, although a great deal of attention may have been put into the implement, if you buy it at a shop, the energy that has been put into it will not have been yours. Making your implements requires you to put this attention into the implement, but only if certain directions are followed.

In his book *Wielding Power*, Charles R. Tetworth sets out directions for the making of magical implements such as a knife, a cup, a wand, and a sword. The idea is to make them with as few resources as possible, partly to reconnect with the aspect of the human mind that remains primitive, but partly also to imbue the objects with the kind of energy that I am talking about here.

Tetworth's directions for making a knife, for example, are very laborious. While you do not have to go to the extent of mining the ore and making the steel for the blade (he advises simply getting a length of mild steel), everything else has to be done from scratch. How do you make a handle? You take strips of bark and glue them to one end of the blade. But where do you get the glue? Not from a store; Tetworth advises getting hold of cow's heels or the skin and bones of some cartilaginous fish such as shark and boiling them down until they turn gluey. The fragrance will not be appealing, but you will have made your own glue rather than having gotten some off the shelf of a shop. Then you tie the handle on for greater firmness. But where do you get the wool? From tufts left by sheep on the bushes of hedgerows. You take these tufts and twist them into yarn, with which you tie the glued strips of bark to the blade. "It requires a degree of commitment and dedication to complete the task, but it will be your work, and no one else's," he says.

As suggested already, it is the quality of attention while doing the work that is important. Tetworth continues:

> When you are . . . performing any action in the making of your weapons, it is vital that you keep your attention wide open. You should be aware of your *breathing*. All your senses should be alert and receptive. You should *hear* every single sound that there is to be heard, *smell* all the scents, *savor* the tastes in the mouth, *see* all there is to see, *feel* every touch on your body and skin—be aware of it all without going off into daydreams or getting caught by any associations that may be triggered. [Emphasis in the original.]

Although I personally have not made ritual implements in this way, I have occasionally used a similar approach in making other things, such as charts of the Kabbalistic Tree of Life. The process is difficult. It requires stopping whenever you are aware that your attention has drifted off or that you are daydreaming, and coming back to the project at hand. In short, it is exactly like the practice of meditation, only in an active, practical context. The end result is not only an object that possesses more of that special aura that I have called "power," but also something inside oneself. Something behind the conscious mind—a seed of will and attention—is formed and, under the right conditions, can continue to grow.

While I could go more deeply into the ideas that I have sketched out here, some of the basic outlines of this particular version of the ancient mystery tradition should be clear by now. It enables one to awaken and wield power in the world—a power that is resourced and quickened by consciousness.

One final note: it is often the custom in articles like this to disguise the names of figures, places, and so on, for the sake of secrecy or discretion. I want to point out that I have not done this. The details that I have described are as I have experienced them.

### SOURCES

Davies, W.G. *The Phoenician Letters.* Manchester, U.K.: Mowat, 1979.

Tetworth, Charles R. *Wielding Power: The Essence of Ritual Practice.* Great Barrington, Mass.: Lindisfarne, 2002.

# Two

# NOSTRADAMUS

NOSTRADAMUS. THE NAME EVOKES the image of a mystical seer dwelling in the half-light of the past, his prophecies coming to us in yellowed volumes that presage disasters in the near distance.

Who was Nostradamus? What did he predict? Could he see the future?

To see what Nostradamus was trying to say and whether his words have meaning for us today, it's helpful to step back and look at him in the context of his times. Although for most people Nostradamus is a shadowy figure, we have a reasonably clear picture of what he was like.

Michel de Nostradamus was born on December 14, 1503, in St.-Rémy-de-Provence in the south of France. His father was a scrivener and attorney named Jacobus de Nostredame, or "James of Our Lady." Originally the family was probably of Jewish origin and took this name as a sign of allegiance to their new Catholic faith. As an adult, Michel would Latinize the surname to "Nostradamus" in the fashion of learned men of his era.

For much of his life, Nostradamus was a wandering scholar, studying and practicing subjects as diverse as medicine, astrology, and even cosmetics and confections. He once made lozenges of rose petals that, he claimed, sweetened the breath and prevented one from getting the plague. (People in those days believed that contagion was spread by noxious odors.)

Only when he was over forty was Nostradamus able to settle down for good. In 1547, he moved to the town of Salon in Provence, in the south of France, and married a rich widow. In 1550, he began to produce an item that was very much in demand at the time: a yearly almanac. In the early sixteenth century, Europe was beset by what climatologists call the "Little Ice Age"—decades of below-average temperatures that played havoc with crops and caused periodic famine. Long-range weather forecasting did not exist in any real sense, and people relied on almanacs, which provided vague weather predictions, to give them some idea of what was coming. Almanacs—including Nostradamus's—also featured prophecies for the coming year.

Although or because Nostradamus's predictions in his

annual almanacs were often vague ("there shall be a great change of condition, almost from top to bottom, and the opposite from bottom to top"), they proved so successful that by 1554, he embarked upon a much more ambitious enterprise: writing a cycle of predictions in quatrains, or four-lined verses. Eventually they would be collected into ten "centuries," or groups of hundred quatrains, which would form the bedrock of his reputation. The collection was entitled *Prophéties* ("Prophecies"). If Nostradamus is quoted today, it's usually from this work.

What did he use to make his predictions? Most likely a combination of three methods. One technique involves *scrying*. This essentially means putting the mind in a meditative state and watching attentively—but without editing or censoring—the images that come up. A second method was *mundane astrology*, which uses the movements and relations of the planets to forecast national and world events. Finally, Nostradamus mined older books of prophecies for his ideas. Since the beginning of Christianity, there has been a vibrant prophetic tradition that tries to take up where the Bible leaves off. Many of these prophecies foretell the coming of a universal Christian monarch to precede Christ's Second Advent. Nostradamus adapted these predictions for his era.

For all the ups and downs that he endured in his early life, in his later years Nostradamus proved astonishingly

fortunate. His greatest piece of luck was Catherine de'
Medici, wife of King Henri II of France. Catherine was a
remarkable and powerful woman who for much of her life
served as a power behind the throne, but she was also an
intense devotee of occultism. Seers, magicians, and astrologers received a warm welcome at her court, and Nostradamus was to be prime among them.

What really cemented Nostradamus's reputation, however, was an event that seemed to fulfill a strangely worded
verse in his *Prophecies*:

> *The young lion will overcome the old one*
> *In a martial field by a duel one on one:*
> *In a cage of gold his eyes will burst:*
> *Two classes one, then to die, cruel death.*

Like most of Nostradamus's verses, this one is abrupt,
cryptic, and broken in its grammar. Nonetheless, it appeared to be strikingly fulfilled with a bizarre disaster
involving King Henri II. Henri was fond of medieval tour-
naments (already an antique affectation in those days) and
enjoyed participating in them himself. In 1559, he jousted
against a young nobleman. The nobleman's lance shattered on Henri's shield; a large splinter went up through
the visor of Henri's helmet, pierced his eye, and lodged in
his brain.

Given the state of surgery in those times, the case was hopeless, and the king died in agony eleven days later. Almost immediately, Nostradamus was credited with predicting the weird accident. The "cage of gold" was the gilded visor of Henri's helmet; the "young lion," his opponent.

Thus Nostradamus's *Prophecies* became required reading. The queen was his greatest supporter, even deigning to visit him at his home in 1564. Nostradamus's career was at its height by the time he died in 1566. One evening he told his secretary, Jean-Aymé de Chavigny, "You will not find me alive at sunrise"—a prediction that proved correct.

Nostradamus's reputation continued to grow after his death. Chavigny republished the full text of the *Prophecies* in 1568 (he is suspected of doctoring some of the verses to improve their accuracy). Since then, these bizarre mystical poems have remained in print—a remarkable feat for a book that is nearly four hundred and fifty years old.

But the seer did not become widely known in the United States until World War II, when the Nazis were making use of him for propaganda. Several of Nostradamus's quatrains speak of "Hister"—an ancient name for the Danube River. For Nostradamus, this name almost certainly meant the Austrian Hapsburg monarchy, in his day one of the great powers of Europe. But the Nazis exploited this detail to predict the triumph of Hitler, who came from Austria and whose name looks very much like "Hister."

The Nazis' propaganda worked so well that the Allies had to produce their own Nostradamus propaganda in response. During the war, MGM made four movies about Nostradamus. Since those days, he has been a standard feature of the popular landscape. His name is splashed over the more imaginative tabloids—usually in connection with predictions that have nothing to do with anything he really said. He has become such a standard feature of the popular mind that immediately after the 9/11 calamity, the most common word searched for on the Internet was "Nostradamus."

But what did he really predict? Let's see what he said in the quatrain that supposedly foretold 9/11:

> *Forty-five degrees, the sky will burn,*
> *Fire to approach the great new city.*
> *Instantly a great scattered flame will leap up,*
> *When one will want to make proof of the Normans.*

By this interpretation, the "new city" is New York, situated at 42 degrees north latitude (close enough to 45 degrees to satisfy many). Even the reference to "making proof of the Normans" seems to fit, since many Americans felt that the "Normans"—i.e., the French—did not support the United States sufficiently in its antiterrorist efforts afterward.

Most likely, though, Nostradamus was thinking of other cities closer to home. A prime candidate is Naples, whose original Greek name, Neapolis, literally means "new city." Naples is close to Mount Vesuvius, an active volcano whose eruption buried the Roman cities of Pompeii and Herculaneum in 79 A.D. If we take this verse at face value, it seems to be predicting a volcanic disaster for Naples. (Naples is at 40 degrees north latitude, but as astrologers of his day complained, Nostradamus was not always careful in calculations.) Although Vesuvius has erupted continually since Nostradamus's time (the most recent episode was in 1944), Naples itself so far has been spared. Alternatively, Nostradamus could be thinking of one of many cities in France called Villeneuve (also meaning "new city"), which are closer to the 45-degree parallel.

By the way, the quatrain above is a literal translation of what Nostradamus actually wrote. Soon after 9/11, a number of versions of this prophecy started to circulate on the Internet, some of them combining parts of this verse with others taken out of context, some of them made up wholesale. These versions can be found by looking for "Urban Legends" on the Web, which is exactly what they are.

Nevertheless, Nostradamus's reputation would not be

so indestructible unless he had some apparent successes. And he did. Many of these involve England, a country Nostradamus probably never visited and with which he otherwise doesn't seem to concern himself. One example:

> *The fortress near the Thames*
> *Will fall when the king is locked inside.*
> *Near the bridge he will be seen in a shirt.*
> *One in front dead, then in the fort barred up.*

The striking part of this verse is the reference to an imprisoned king who is "seen in a shirt." King Charles I of England, deposed by a popular revolution, was publicly beheaded in London in January 1649. He famously said before his execution, "Let me have a shirt more than ordinary, by reason the season is so sharp as probably make me shake [*sic*], which some will imagine proceeds from fear. I would have no such imputation."

Even so, the connection isn't that clear. The king was not executed "near the bridge"—that is, London Bridge, the only one in the city at the time—but two miles away. Other details in the quatrains don't fit the episode as well. This situation, where one or two details seem very striking but the rest of the verse doesn't make a great deal of sense in the same context, is true of practically all of Nostradamus's prophecies, even the more successful ones.

Considering all this, we can ask, what was Nostradamus's real agenda? Overall, he probably did not have one. He had tried many occupations, including doctor and confectioner, before hitting on one that made him a success. It's also true that he thought of himself as a seer and a magus, and like most such men he never ceased delving into life's mysteries. He was lucky to have hit upon an occupation that enabled to him to pursue his interests while also bestowing fame and prosperity.

Even so, we do see the general outlines of a prophetic direction in Nostradamus. He keeps returning to the theme of a coming universal Christian monarch, as in this verse:

> Like a gryphon will come the king of Europe,
> Accompanied by those of Aquilon,
> Of reds and whites he will lead a great troop,
> And they will go against the king of Babylon.

Here the "king of Europe" probably refers to this universal monarch; "Aquilon," from the Latin word for the North Wind, figuratively refers to the north. Since biblical times, "Babylon" has symbolized spiritual wickedness or apostasy. In this case "the king of Babylon" probably refers to the sultan of the Ottoman Empire (today's Turkey), who in Nostradamus's day ruled over Mesopotamia, including the abandoned city of Babylon. The sultan was also head of the Muslims, who to Christians in those days were infidels, so the name fit in this sense as well.

Many of Nostradamus's other forecasts allude to a coming Muslim invasion of Europe. In a way, this was no prophecy: it was happening in his own time. The European powers were struggling, not always successfully, to keep the Ottomans at bay. In Nostradamus's time, the Ottomans had control of the Balkans and the eastern Mediterranean, and were constantly pushing westward. His verses predict that they will penetrate far into Europe before the great Christian monarch arises to drive them away. Some interpreters of Nostradamus today link these prophecies with the current influx of Muslims into Europe, but the connection does not hold up well. Muslims in countries like France and Germany have for the most part come there peacefully, to work. It is hard to fit them into Nostradamus's views of Turkish hordes sweeping across Europe.

This brings us to a crucial point about Nostradamus's prophecies. They usually make sense in light of the fears and preconceptions of his time; in this context they're often much clearer than they are given credit for. Although he claimed that his prophecies extended to the year 3797 A.D. (it's not clear why he chose this date), most of them seem to be meant for his own day.

Moreover, Nostradamus's prophecies, as we've seen, are vague and allusive. With their broken grammar and cryptic verbiage, they possess a power that can only be called oracular—and oracles are famed for their obscurity. Sometimes he seems almost to be speaking of archetypal situations, much like the texts appended to the hexagrams of the *I Ching*, which can be applied to many circumstances. It's this feature, probably more than any other, that has ensured Nostradamus's popularity.

If Nostradamus's record is so spotty, we might then ask, is it possible to predict the future at all? To answer this question, it's helpful to remember that many spiritual teachings say that reality is ultimately mental in nature: something exists in the realm of thought before it exists in reality. In simple terms, you have to have some idea of the picture you're going to paint before you paint it. But it is said that events, too, exist in a realm of thought before they manifest in the physical world. This, in fact, is why thought has such power: an extremely effective way of changing reality is to change your thoughts about it.

If all this is true, it should theoretically be possible to glimpse events in the world of thought forms before they manifest in reality. This is what most prophecy attempts to do, but in practice it generally doesn't work all that well. To see this for yourself, just go to any shop that sells used books and take a look at works of prophecy that were published ten or twenty years ago. You'll be amazed—but not at their accuracy.

In what sense, then, can we see the future? Many people have premonitions that serve as warnings or guideposts for the time ahead—foretelling an accident, the death of a loved one, and so on. In short, the future is sometimes revealed to us—but usually only in the very short term, and in terms of what affects us personally. Big-picture issues, such as who will win the next election or when the Dow will hit 15,000, are, the unseen realms seem to be saying, none of our business.

This may seem discomfiting today, when we are constantly inundated by warnings of all sorts of disasters, natural and supernatural, supposedly to come. But we don't have to worry. If the past is any guide, practically none of these prophecies will come true. And in any case, the lesson isn't about seeing the future. It *is* about having the inner strength and serenity to know we can deal with whatever the future brings.

## Three

# DOES PROPHECY WORK?

ELIE WIESEL, IN HIS SOMBER memoir *Night*, describes a poignant incident from his time in a Nazi concentration camp. Amidst unimaginable suffering and despair, an inmate named Akiba Drumer "had discovered a verse from the Bible, which, translated into numbers, made it possible for him to predict Redemption in the weeks to come."

There have been countless Akiba Drumers over the last two thousand years. Confronting dismal memories of the past and the bleak actualities of the present, they have turned to the future for hope and solace.

The trend is not necessarily as old as humanity itself. While traditional mythologies ranging from those of the Hindus to those of the ancient Germans spoke of the rising and passing of ages in cycles, the Abrahamic religions—Judaism, Christianity, and Islam—have tended to see history as aimed toward a final destination point, an end of time in which the ledger books of justice will be balanced and all of humanity will be marched off to salvation or perdition. This is sometimes called the Apocalypse, and literature devoted to it is called "apocalyptic."

What exactly is prophecy? Can we trust it?

The esoteric tradition—the body of knowledge that underlies all the great spiritual traditions of humanity—teaches that the future is, at least in principle, knowable. There are several theories to account for such events (and they are not mutually exclusive). One of these holds that there exists a realm of images and forms, which has many names in many traditions. The Kabbalists call it the world of Yetzirah, or "formation"; quite possibly it is what Australian aborigines call the Dreaming and what some Western occultists refer to as the astral realm. This realm of images does not exist in any physical sense, but all the same it has a reality of its own. If you think of a lightbulb, say, that image in your mind has some reality, even some substance, although not physically.

Esotericism also teaches that this world of images is *prior to* the physical world: events and things manifest in this realm before they appear in palpable reality. Consequently, someone with reasonably clear access to this dimension—deliberately, through divination or prophetic contemplation, or spontaneously, through dreams or hunches or intuitions—should be able to see the future.

Some readers may wonder what this theory may have to do with synchronicity, a concept that is often invoked when people attempt to understand such forms of divination as the Tarot or the *I Ching*. "Synchronicity" in this sense is a coinage of the Swiss psychologist C. G. Jung, who defines it as an "acausal connecting principle." Jung gives a case in point: "The wife of one of my patients, a man in his fifties, once told me in conversation that, at the deaths of her mother and her grandmother, a number of birds gathered outside the windows of the death-chamber." Such incidents are common: I can tell similar stories from my own family. For Jung, the connection between these events—the deaths and the appearance of the birds—is not causal; that is, the impending death didn't cause the birds to come or vice versa. But they are related by what he calls a "meaningful cross-connection."

Jung's attempt to characterize synchronicity as "acausal" appears misguided. He seems to be veering toward a connection that is not acausal in the strict sense; rather, it implies a hidden factor lying outside the physical dimension that, so to speak, "caused" both the death and the appearances of the birds. Jung locates this hidden cause in the realm of the archetypes, the psychic forces that underlie the human mind and possibly reality itself. For Jung, "meaningful coincidences . . . seem to have an archetypal foundation."

Granting this much, we are left with a theory very close to the esoteric doctrine sketched out above. Jung's archetypal world is more or less identical to the realm of Yetzirah, of forms and images. As such, it can give rise to two phenomena that have no obvious causal relation (such as a death and the sudden appearance of a flock of birds) and yet seem to be meaningfully connected. Jung made much of being scientific, and to a great degree he was—but his conclusions in many respects resemble those of the old occultists.

Another esoteric theory about seeing the future is based on the highly relative nature of time. Time, as Immanuel Kant argued, is one of the basic structural components of our experience, but it is a construct that our minds have imposed on reality. As hard as it may be to imagine, time has no absolute reality in itself (a conclusion to which contemporary physics may also point). If so, it may be possible to step past the portals of our own experiential framework and take some measure of events in the future.

Many spiritual traditions speak of a higher Self, a part of our being that stands over and above our selves as we customarily experience them. The names for this Self are countless. The ancient Greeks called it the *daimon*; the ancient Romans, the *genius*; to esoteric Christians, it is the kingdom of heaven or the Christ within. This Self stands outside the personality, the conscious self, and outside the categories of conscious experience, including time. It perceives our lives, not as a sequence of events and experiences that span several decades, but as a whole. It can see a lifetime as we can see a snapshot.

A famous instance of the workings of this Self appears in the *Crito* of Plato. Socrates, under sentence of execution, is urged to escape by his rich friend Crito, who assures him that he has bribed the guards and can furnish the necessary getaway. Socrates refuses, saying he has had a dream in which a beautiful woman dressed in white appeared to him and recited a line from the *Iliad*: "On the third day to the fertile land of Phthia thou shalt come." Socrates takes this as a message from his *daimon*, the guiding spirit that has directed him all throughout his life, that he will be executed in three days, and that he should not try to escape. One way of understanding such episodes is that the *daimon*, the Self, can see the whole of one's life from start to finish, apart from the linearity of time, and can give appropriate guidance.

Note, however, that, as in Socrates' case, these glimpses usually have to do with one's deeper destiny. It's not a question of picking next week's lottery number or finding hot stocks. While these are in principle no more unknowable than anything else, one soon discovers that the higher Self is not terribly interested in them—and anyway, how helpful would the knowledge really be? I know directly of only one case where someone got this kind of information. A friend of my father's once told me he had been awakened in the middle of the night by the image of some numbers that flashed in his mind. It struck him that they might be lottery numbers and that he should buy a ticket using them, but he never got around to it. Of course they were the winning numbers that week.

If these visions of the future are ultimately personal in nature—that is, they are meant to give guidance or inspiration to an individual at crucial junctures in his or her life—what then of prophecy in a grander sense, the prophecy that purports to open a window onto the fates of nations and peoples, and of humanity itself?

As a whole, the record of prophecy in predicting the future on a large scale is not good. We can see this as far back as the start of the apocalyptic genre in Palestine in the second century B.C. At the time, the Jewish nation was living under the rule of the Hellenistic Seleucid monarchs, who were heirs to a portion of the empire of Alexander the Great. In 167 B.C., one of these rulers, Antiochus IV Ephiphanes, embarked on a program of forced Hellenization of the Jews. He set up an altar, and perhaps an image, of Olympian Zeus in the Temple in Jerusalem.

The Jews' outrage is reflected in the Book of Daniel, one of the earliest apocalyptic writings and the only one to make its way into the Hebrew Bible. Written during the ensuing revolt against the Seleucids, this book sets up Daniel, a legendary sage of the sixth century B.C., as the mouthpiece of a prophecy that would "foretell" events four hundred years after his time. (The technical term for this practice is *vaticinium ex eventu*, "prediction from the event.") Daniel refers to "a vile person"—Antiochus—who will "pollute the sanctuary of strength, and shall take away the daily sacrifice, and . . . shall place the abomination that maketh desolate" (Dan. 11:21, 31)—that is, the idol in the Temple (cf. 1 Macc. 1:54). The Archangel Michael will come to Israel's rescue; the dead will be raised, "some to everlasting life, and some to shame and everlasting contempt." Antiochus "shall come to his end, and none shall help him" (Dan. 11:45, 12:1–2).

What happened in fact was that the Jews rose up under the priestly clan of the Maccabees and won back their religious liberties as well as a measure of political autonomy, but this obviously did not begin the end of time. Antiochus did not perish as a result of any obvious divine wrath: he died of natural causes.

Despite its failure as prophecy, the Book of Daniel established the basic structure of the apocalyptic genre. Arising during some crisis, such texts predict that this event is the harbinger of the imminent Day of Judgment, when justice will be done and evildoers will receive their due. The Book of Revelation at the end of the New Testament follows this pattern. Most scholars agree that it is a response to the Roman persecution of Christians in the first century A.D. Here, too, the prophecy, taken as literal truth, is not accurate. The book seems to foretell the end of the Roman Empire and the coming of a millennial kingdom, but this did not happen. The Roman Empire *did* come to an end (close to four hundred years after Revelation was written), but it did not usher in the reign of God on earth. Rather it initiated a period of collapse and chaos that came to be known as the Dark Ages.

Even the prophecies of Jesus as related in the Gospels do not seem trustworthy. If we are to read what scholars call his Apocalyptic Discourse literally (three versions of it appear in Matthew 24, Mark 13, and Luke 21), we would conclude that he was predicting the destruction of the Temple by the Romans, to be followed by the return of the Son of God. This did not happen either. The Romans did sack the Temple, in 70 A.D., about a generation after Jesus's lifetime, but Jesus did not return and did not establish a millennial kingdom. Things went on much as they had (except for the Jews, who were expelled from Palestine).

I'm using instances from the Bible as it is by far the best-known work of prophecy, but if we were to look at prophecies from other sources, they would not look much better. The American trance medium Edgar Cayce foretold that much of California would be under water by

1972. Nostradamus predicted some kind of great manifestation in the sky for the seventh month of 1999, but the year 1999 had very little that was remarkable, much less cataclysmic, either in the seventh or in any other month.

How, then, can we reconcile the abysmal performance of prophecy as a whole with the esoteric theory that I've sketched out above? If we *can* know the future, why don't we?

The astral realm is a sea of images. We can think of it as containing every image and idea that every human being has ever thought and possibly will ever think. No sooner do we say this than we realize that this dimension must contain an enormous amount of psychic rubbish— the fears, dreads, and anxieties of humanity, most of which have nothing to do with reality past or present. This dimension is described most clearly in the spiritual text known as *A Course in Miracles*:

> The circle of fear lies just below the level the body sees, and seems to be the whole foundation on which the world is based. Here are all the illusions, all the twisted thoughts, all the insane attacks, the fury, the vengeance and betrayal that were made to keep the guilt in place, so that the world could rise from it and keep it hidden. Its shadow rises to the

surface, enough to hold its most external manifestations in darkness, and to bring despair and loneli-
ness to it and keep it joyless.

Without going into the elaborate psychological system of
the *Course*, I will simply point to the notion of the "circle of
fear"—a zone of fears, hatreds, and anxieties that lies just
below the surface of consciousness. This circle of fear is
universal: each of us participates in its creation. Probably
only the most enlightened human beings are entirely free
from its effects. For the rest of us, it sits underneath our
experience of reality like a water table. We all tap into it in
our own ways.

This fear is not "about" anything particular; it is not
necessarily connected to anything real or substantial; it is
simply a nameless, objectless anxiety that can attach itself
to anything. It holds tremendous power over each of us
precisely because we are usually unconscious of it. We
imagine that our fears and anxieties are about something
real and justified, but there is something suspect about this
belief: no sooner does one anxiety disappear than another
pops up to take its place. For many people, this anxiety can
manifest in fears about their personal future or about society or humanity or the earth; for others, it is displaced
onto a fear of an imminent end of the world.

Some say fear is a healthy and normal emotion, that without it we could not function. This may be true under certain circumstances. If a man finds himself facing a wild animal, his fear will make him run away. But the kind of fear I am talking about is not healthy. It does not increase our chances for survival; instead it is weakening and debilitating. Much of mental dysfunction no doubt stems from too close a contact with this kind of fear.

Saying this much explains the horrific imagery of so many prophecies, but what about the nice part? What about the beautiful dreams of a utopian future that is always just around the horizon? The explanation is the same. The Yetziratic or astral realm is known to esotericists as the "zone of illusion." We can think of it as a bandwidth of fantasies and illusions that surrounds us on a psychic level. While many of these fantasies are negative, there are also many that are positive; they are the flip side of the circle of fear. The power of wishful thinking—which is very strong—can easily lead someone to put all these images together into a picture of the future that involves both terrible calamities (usually visited on one's enemies) and ultimate salvation (for oneself and one's own sect). Akiba Drumer's prophecy in the concentration camp most likely falls into this category.

Our age imagines itself to be more sophisticated than its predecessors, and yet the contemporary mind falls prey to many of the temptations of the past. Cataclysmic and millennialistic thinking is as much with us as ever. The religious-minded cast it in biblical images. The secular mindset translates it into visions of nuclear or environmental disaster. The problems posed by both nuclear power and environmental contamination are very great and should not be dismissed out of hand, but it is also well to separate them from unconscious apocalyptic expectations, which can erupt from the minds of supposedly rational scientists just as easily as they can from men wearing sandwich boards on street corners.

Having said this much, we might want to compare prophecy with prediction of a more conventional kind, which has evolved into an academic discipline (or pseudo-discipline) known as futurology. Futurology makes no supernatural assumptions. It is based entirely on what is currently known. It takes current statistics—about population, economic growth, political trends, resource capacity—and extrapolates them into the future. That is its strength but also its weakness. Futurology can only make predictions on the basis of current trends, but one thing we know is that current trends never continue. There are shocks, dislocations, cataclysms. Conventional forecasters cannot predict these; their unpredictability is at the root of their nature.

The apocalyptic prophet faces no such restrictions. He

has no incentive to predict more of the same; who would pay attention to him then? So he is entirely happy to foretell all kinds of upheavals, natural and supernatural: the submerging of continents; the manifestation of extraterrestrials; the shifting of the earth's pole; the return of Jesus Christ. In a sense, he is right. Cataclysms do occur. But somehow they never occur in the way they were predicted.

In the end, I personally would not base my plans for the future on any prophetic claims from any source. I can't say that none of these prophecies will be fulfilled—that would be making a prophecy of my own—but to my mind they haven't been proved reliable enough in the past to merit any serious attention now. Conventional futurology may offer some insights, but frequently it, too, better represents the analyst's preconceptions than any reality that is likely to come.

All this still leaves us with the possibility of a knowable future, whose seeds are present in the astral realm amidst all the fears and fantasies. How can we have contact with it? Trying to glimpse the future on a collective level is extremely tricky, often because it is something into which we as individuals are not supposed to stick our noses.

When we come to the personal future, the situation is different. I myself have often found that when I needed to be told of something that was going to happen to me, I was informed of it, usually through some form of inner perception, bidden or unbidden. I have not found divination methods like the Tarot or the *I Ching* to be particularly useful. Astrology, on the other hand, can have remarkable predictive value—provided one knows the system well enough to understand what the stars are saying.

These are my conclusions from my own experience. Others may have different results; these matters are more individual than popular books like to let on. In the end, for me nothing has proved to be of as much value as a clear-sighted determination to see what was going on both inside and outside myself, to look upon my own hopes and fears and wishes, and to bring them face to face to what Freud called "the reality principle." A. R. Orage, a pupil of the great spiritual teacher G. I. Gurdjieff, defined "conscience" in a rather unusual way as "the simultaneous experience of all one's emotions." If you can do this with a naked and even remorseless honesty (and it is considerably harder than it may first seem), you are far more likely to have an accurate basis for future action than if you follow the advice of any number of psychics or prophets.

# Four

# SECRETS OF
# *THE DA VINCI CODE*

A CURATOR AT THE LOUVRE, imperfectly murdered by an albino monk, realizes he has fifteen minutes to live. In the time remaining to him, he scrawls a series of enigmatic clues to his fate on his body and on artworks in the museum. These clues draw the curator's granddaughter Sophie, along with a Harvard cryptographer named Robert Langdon, into an elaborate adventure to solve the crime and, incidentally, to unveil the best-kept secret of the past two thousand years.

This tale forms the plot of Dan Brown's novel *The Da Vinci Code*, which has become a publishing phenomenon since it first appeared in April 2003. As even the sketchiest outline suggests, *The Da Vinci Code* is a thriller. It overflows with last-minute escapes, high-tech surveillance, ruthless thugs, and sinister conspiracies at the highest circles of power.

None of these devices—which by now have gone past cliché and at this point simply form part of the basic vocabulary of the genre—accounts for the astounding success of *The Da Vinci Code*. Even unsophisticated readers complain of its cardboard characters and improbable plot twists. The book's popularity can only be explained by the appeal of its subject matter. The crime and its solution have nothing to do with drug rings, underworld lords, or political chicaneries. Instead they involve the Catholic Church, a reactionary Catholic organization known as Opus Dei, a mysterious secret society called the Priory of Sion, and the quest for the Holy Grail—not to mention Mary Magdalene and Jesus Christ himself.

During the frantic chases and close escapes of *The Da Vinci Code*, the hero and heroine unearth an astonishing revelation: Jesus Christ was not the celibate we have been led to believe. In fact, following standard practice for Jewish men then and now, he was married. His wife was Mary Magdalene, and their offspring survived to form the bloodline of the Merovingian dynasty, which ruled France from the fifth through the eighth centuries. The Catholic Church, with its horror of anything that might connect the feminine with the divine, did its best to repress this fact, but it was always preserved underground. During the Crusades, the secret was entrusted to the Knights Templar, who used it to blackmail the Catholic Church into granting the Templars virtually limitless power. The Church bided its time, however, and managed to suppress the Templars in the fourteenth century. At this point the secret was passed on to the Priory of Sion, an order that numbered among its leaders Isaac Newton, Victor Hugo, and of course Leonardo da Vinci. The Priory guards it up to the present (or at least up to the time of the novel), intending, perhaps, to reveal the truth to the world in the current era.

This aspect of the plot makes the novel's success much easier to understand. The Templars, the Priory of Sion, the Catholic Church, Mary Magdalene are all proven sales successes. So, of course, is Jesus himself. American newsmagazines like *Time* and *U.S. News and World Report*, finding that issues featuring Jesus outsell practically all others, constantly put the carpenter of Nazareth on their covers, usually to announce some amazing new "facts" about his life that turn out not to be news at all. So it was a brilliant stroke on Dan Brown's part to take these themes and offer them in the easy-to-swallow form of a suspense novel.

*The Da Vinci Code* is a work of fiction, of course, and Brown would be within his rights to have made up every last detail in it. But much of the material that forms the core of the mystery in his book is based on real or alleged fact. The story about the sacred bloodline of Jesus and Mary Magdalene—as well as its preservation in the Merovingian dynasty—is, as Brown acknowledges, taken from the best-seller *Holy Blood, Holy Grail* by Richard Leigh, Henry Lincoln, and Michael Baigent. Opus Dei really exists—as does the Priory of Sion (though not in the form described). So it would be interesting to see how much factuality there is in *The Da Vinci Code*. As usually happens, the truth is both more interesting and more complicated than a novel can make it appear.

A careful reading of the novel suggests that Brown has, as he claims, done a considerable amount of research. Unfortunately, his research often tends to be wrong. He claims, for example, that "the Bible, as we know it today, was collated by the pagan Roman emperor Constantine the Great."

There is really no truth to this assertion. The Old Testament canon was established by Jewish rabbis and sages in a process that culminated in the two councils of Jamnia in A.D. 90 and 118, two centuries before Constantine. And while the final canon of the New Testament was not set until the fourth century, when Constantine lived, there is no evidence that the emperor himself set it. It *is* true that the first list of the twenty-seven books of the New Testament that are now recognized as canonical appears in a letter of the fourth-century Church Father Athanasius, whose views on the Trinity had prevailed at the Council of Nicaea in A.D. 325, which Constantine had convened.

But this is far from saying that the emperor "collated" the Bible as we know it today.

Brown also says that Mary Magdalene was a descendant of the "House of Benjamin," and that Jesus's marriage to her created a dynastic link between the House of Benjamin and the House of David. It is certainly correct to say that Jesus belonged, or was believed to belong, to the House of David; the Gospels frequently allude to this lineage. But there was no House of Benjamin. Benjamin was a small tribe that had been incorporated into the biblical kingdom of Judah, and while Saul, Israel's first king, was of the tribe of Benjamin (1 Sam. 9:1–2), there is no evidence that this line survived to Christ's time or that Mary Magdalene was part of it.

Mary Magdalene's role in *The Da Vinci Code* deserves further examination. As Brown indicates, she was not the penitent whore of later Catholic hagiography. Over the centuries she became conflated with "the woman taken in adultery" who appears in the eighth chapter of John, but there is no reason to believe that she was the same woman, and every reason to believe she was not: otherwise John would have said so, since he mentions Mary Magdalene elsewhere. We know only two things about Mary Magdalene from the canonical Gospels, summarized in Mark 16:9: "Now when Jesus was risen early the first day of the

*Secrets of* The Da Vinci Code  ✦  53

week, he appeared first to Mary Magdalene, out of whom he had cast seven devils."

These facts—that Christ first appeared to Mary Magdalene and that he had cast seven devils out of her—are not as unrelated as they may appear. But they only make sense in terms of the symbolic language in which the Bible was written, and which has always been known and understood in esoteric Christianity.

The number seven is key here. Ancient cosmology saw the earth as surrounded by the spheres of the seven planets as then known: the moon, Mercury, Venus, the sun, Mars, Jupiter, and Saturn. The spiritual forces of these planets were portrayed by ancient esoteric traditions, including Hermeticism and Gnosticism, as malign gatekeepers of the heavenly realms, who sought to keep man bound to earth. They are, in fact, the "rulers of the darkness of this world" mentioned in Ephesians 6:12. The liberation of the soul was seen as an ascent through the seven spheres and an undoing of the bonds of these malign planetary powers. Thus one who is liberated could be described as having had "seven devils" cast out of her. In its figurative language, the Gospel seems to be saying that the "second birth" of the spirit, symbolized by the Resurrection, is attained first and foremost by one who has transcended the influences of the planets, that is, by one out of whom "seven devils" have been cast.

These considerations reinforce the high status that Mary Magdalene had in early Christianity. As the messenger of the Resurrection, she was known as "the Apostle to the Apostles." But was she Christ's wife?

Two facts cast some light on this question. One is an extremely peculiar passage in the apocryphal Gospel of Philip:

> The companion of the [Savior is] Mary Magdalene. [But Christ loved her] more than [all] the disciples [and used to] kiss her [often] on her [mouth.] The rest of [the disciples were offended] by it [and expressed disapproval.] They said to him, "Why do you love her more than all of us?" The Savior answered and said to them, "Why do I not love you like her?" (Bracketed words have been added by the translator.)

The answer to this question is, presumably, obvious.

The Gospel of Philip, like most apocryphal Gospels, is comparatively late (dated to the second half of the third century) and is not necessarily an accurate biographical account. But some writers have pointed out another interesting fact. Mary Magdalene was the first to appear at the tomb on the third day because it was her task to anoint the body of Jesus. It is possible that this was because she was his wife, since it would naturally fall to close family members to perform this task, since the ancient Jews were intensely concerned about being defiled with the dead. "He that toucheth the dead body of any man shall be unclean for seven days" (Num. 19:11). (This, by the way, is why the priest and the Levite pass by the man waylaid by robbers in the parable of the Good Samaritan.) It would stand to reason that the task of preparing the body for burial would fall to the dead man's closest relations— notably his wife.

While these details are intriguing, they don't add up to proof that Jesus and Mary Magdalene were married. And such proof does not exist. On the other hand, the absence of proof does not constitute refutation. Brown is right in pointing out, as he often does, that the official Church did its best to suppress any documents that might cast doubt upon its own portrayal of Christ. Given the amount of material that has been lost from antiquity even apart from official suppression, it would come more as a surprise that any such evidence existed than if it did not.

There is even less evidence that Christ and Mary Magdalene had children. I do not know of any allusions to this possibility in either the canonical or apocryphal Gospels. The only reference to it I have come across, apart from material based directly or indirectly on *Holy Blood, Holy Grail*, was in a 1998 interview I did with the British occultist R. J. Stewart. He told me, "One of the 'secret' things that was taught in the English lodges—which is now quite widespread, but I heard this in the 1960s, when no one publicized anything like it—was that the Grail was embodied in a son and a daughter of Jesus by Mary Magdalene." Stewart went on to say that these were known esoterically as "the vessel and two cruets, one containing the blood and one containing the sweat of Jesus—sometimes thought to be a euphemism for seed, for semen." The "vessel" and "cruets" were supposedly brought to England by Joseph of Arimathea after Christ's death.

But Stewart did not seem to think this implied that Christ's offspring left any descendants, still less that these descendants went on to form the bloodline of the kings of France. "These claims that kings of certain lines are descended from the blood of Jesus, in my opinion, are probably modern," he said. "It just seems to me that the whole [medieval] culture was not about overt lineage from Jesus for kings. It was more about some sacred embodiment of kingship, a divine right of kings, that was older than Christianity."

The issue of sacred kingship takes us to the heart of the matter. It raises the question of the alleged divine bloodline of Jesus, and who would find it in their interest to propound such an idea in the absence of any real evidence. The most convincing argument I have seen in this regard comes from a writer named Robert Richardson, who argues in great detail that the Priory of Sion, allegedly a secret society entrusted for centuries with protecting the Grail and the secret of the divine bloodline, does in fact exist. It is not, however, an ancient esoteric order, but the creation of ultra-right-wing French monarchists of the twentieth century. (Richardson discusses his findings in the article "The Priory of Sion Fraud," in *Gnosis* 51 [Spring 1999].)

According to Richardson's research, there was once an authentic Catholic order called the Priory of Sion. Originally centered in Palestine, it later transferred its headquarters to Sicily. But it ceased to exist in 1617, being absorbed into the Jesuit order. The modern "Priory of Sion" was the creation of a Frenchman named Pierre Plantard. Born in 1920, Plantard became influential in his late teens as a leader of Catholic youth groups. Around the outbreak of World War II, he became titular head of an alleged esoteric order named Alpha Galates. During the German occupation in the early 1940s, Plantard and Alpha Galates published a newspaper called *Vaincre* ("Conquer"). *Vaincre* was pro-German and anti-Semitic, combining its political messages with discussions of Celtic esoterica and chivalry. It published only six issues.

After the war, Plantard began to promote himself as the heir to the Merovingian dynasty, and in 1956, to further this end, he founded an organization called the "Priory of Sion," which had no connection with the extinct Catholic order. In the 1950s and 1960s, Plantard and his organization promoted a mélange of anti-Semitic, anti-Masonic views while espousing a rightist view of French nationalism.

All of this may seem mystifying to the English-speaking reader, for whom this blend of intrigue, conspiracy, and manipulation may seem better suited to a thriller than to reality. But in fact there are some major differences between the esoteric climate of the English-speaking world and that of the European continent. In Britain, America, and the Commonwealth, esoteric lodges have long followed the lead of Grand Lodge Masonry, which promoted liberal ideals in the eighteenth and nineteenth centuries and has long been (for better or worse) a mainstay of the status quo. Members of the British royal family have long been titular heads of the Grand Lodge of England, and a number of U.S. presidents have been high-degree Masons.

In continental Europe the situation has been different. The power of the Catholic Church—and its long-standing aversion to secret societies of any type, whether or not they professed loyalty to the Church—spawned Masonic groups that were revolutionary and anticlerical. In response or reaction, occult orders arose that were intended to guard the privileges of Church and nobility against the inroads of bourgeois republicans. In the nineteenth and twentieth centuries, these groups became drawn toward nationalistic, fascistic, and monarchistic ideals. Among such groups is, apparently, the Priory of Sion. As Robert Richardson observes,

> The "Priory"'s first objective is to position itself in the mind of an unknowing public as the supreme Western esoteric organization. It dreams of utilizing that constituency in a synarchy-like fashion to promote its hybrid agenda of right-wing politics and turn-of-the-century esoteric teachings. It does not represent the real teachings of any positive esoteric order. It is materialistic, obsessed with attaining influence, and has fabricated documents without regard for any ethical considerations. Its program is to manipulate people through lies in order to promote itself.

In the early years of the twenty-first century, when the chicaneries and dishonesties of world political leaders have become ever more glaring, the threats posed by a Priory of Sion can hardly seem terrifying. But it is interesting to note how its claims have made their way to a wide audience, first in *Holy Blood, Holy Grail*, and now in *The Da Vinci Code*. The latter tells us that the surnames of the descendants of the Merovingians—and hence of Jesus too—were Plantard and Saint-Clair. Thus we see Plantard's claim to divine lineage vindicated in the pages of a popular novel.

It is interesting to note the other surname Brown gives: Saint-Clair. In the first place, the real-life Pierre Plantard claimed that *his* original surname was St. Clair. But according to Richardson, this, too, is a hoax. Plantard was laying claim to the name of the St. Clair or Sinclair family, Scottish nobles who were the hereditary protectors of Freemasonry as well as proprietors of a chapel at Rosslyn, near Edinburgh. Rosslyn, the site where Brown's novel reaches its climax, is renowned among connoisseurs of esoteric lore. One of the more fascinating (if inconclusive) parts of *Holy Blood, Holy Grail* argues that the curious imagery of its stonework make it a kind of missing link between the Templars and the Freemasons.

By this theory, some of the Templars, fleeing persecution by the Catholic Church on the European continent at the beginning of the fourteenth century, made their way to Scotland, where they helped the new king, Robert the Bruce, repel an English invasion. Here they went underground for three centuries (constructing the Rosslyn chapel in the meantime) until they surfaced at the turn of the seventeenth century in the guise of Masonic lodges, which originated in Scotland and spread to England in the early seventeenth century.

The connection between the Templars and the Freemasons is more persuasive than much of the story I have dealt with so far. There *are* esoteric orders that go underground to preserve their teachings for hundreds of years at a time, surfacing when events call for their presence. One well-known example was the Rosicrucian Brotherhood, which made its appearance felt in the public eye in the seventeenth century and provided an initial impetus toward the Scientific Revolution and toward republican government; later incarnations appeared in eighteenth-century Prussia, nineteenth-century France, and twentieth-century America. But there is no evidence that any of these organizations were devoted to preserving the lineage of a sacred monarchy, and much to suggest that they were not.

*The Da Vinci Code* gives a complex and ambiguous picture of the Catholic Church. Opus Dei, the cultlike Catholic society that has achieved increasing influence over the past twenty years, appears in an unmitigatedly negative light. Silas, the albino monk who murders the Louvre curator, is portrayed as performing intense self-mortifications such as flogging and wearing the cilice, a spiked chain that Opus Dei members wear for two hours a day as a form of penance. Silas's penchant for murder is portrayed as the consequence of unquestioning obedience to his superiors—an attitude fostered by the real Opus Dei. The novel also says Opus Dei gained its power by bailing out the Vatican bank during its financial scandals in 1982. The official Opus Dei Web site (www.opusdei.org) responds:

> The Da Vinci Code . . . gives a bizarre and inaccurate portrayal of the Catholic institution Opus Dei. The numerous inaccuracies range from simple factual errors to outrageous and false depictions of criminal or pathological behavior. For example, the novel depicts members of Opus Dei practicing gruesome corporal mortifications and murdering people, implies that Opus Dei coerces or brainwashes people, suggests that Opus Dei has drugged new members to induce religious experiences, and insinuates that Opus Dei bailed out the Vatican bank in return for its establishment as a personal prelature. All of this is absurd nonsense.

Brown, for his part, claims that his picture of Opus Dei was based on factual research. "I worked very hard to create a fair and balanced depiction of Opus Dei," he claims on his personal Web site (www.danbrown.com), adding that he based his account on published works about the organization as well as personal interviews with current and former members. Reporter Paul Moses, in an article in the New York newspaper *Newsday*, indicates that while some of the more extreme forms of behavior in the novel (presumably including murder) are exaggerated, others, such as wearing the cilice, are accurate, and self-flagellation is not unknown.

In *The Da Vinci Code*, the Catholic Church disowns Opus Dei as "a liability and an embarrassment" for its outmoded understanding of Christianity. This is an action Pope John Paul II (who was pope at the time of *The Da Vinci Code*'s publication) was unlikely to take; in fact Opus Dei's founder, a Spanish priest named Josemaría Escrivá, was canonized in 2002. Hence the novel portrays a Catholic Church under a new, more liberal and enlightened pope dedicated to "updating Catholicism into the third millennium"—an implicit criticism of the Vatican's leadership at the time.

Most crucially, however, the Catholic Church is portrayed as an enemy of the Divine Feminine. In the end, the secret of the Grail has less to do with the sacred bloodline than with the holiness of the feminine, which, Brown tells us, the Church has constantly denied and denigrated.

Taken at face value, this idea is absurd. The Virgin Mary is a central figure in Catholic devotion—for many believers, far more vivid and immediate than God the

Father or Christ himself. To quote an article from the British newsmagazine *The Economist*, a visitor entering a church with no prior knowledge of Christianity during Christmastime "might well conclude that the main person being celebrated and adored was not a newborn boy, but his mother." As one reader on the Amazon.com Web site grumbled about *The Da Vinci Code*, "The anti-Catholic bias of this nonsense reaches ridiculous proportions. I mean, come on: for the last five centuries we have been taught that the Catholic Church was evil precisely because it had PERPETUATED goddess worship in the form of the cult of Mary and the saints. Now we are supposed to believe that the Catholic Church is evil for exactly the opposite reason, that it SUPPRESSED goddess worship?"

But the point goes beyond the issue of mere goddess worship. It is true that the Catholic Church deems Mary worthy of a veneration only slightly less than is due to God himself. Historical evidence suggests that the proclamation of Mary as Theotokos or "Mother of God" in the fifth century A.D. was partly intended to fill the vacuum left by the suppression of the worship of Isis, the all-compassionate Egyptian mother goddess popular in the Greco-Roman world. But Mary is a *virgin* goddess. And here lies the crux of the issue. Brown puts these words into the mouth of his hero:

For the early Church, . . . mankind's use of sex to commune directly with God posed a serious threat to the Catholic power base. It left the Church out of the loop, undermining their self-proclaimed status as the *sole* conduit to God. For obvious reasons, they worked hard to demonize sex and recast it as a disgusting and sinful act. . . . Is it surprising we feel conflicted about sex? . . . Our ancient heritage and our very physiologies tell us sex is natural—a cherished route to spiritual fulfillment—and yet modern religion decries it as shameful, teaching us to fear our sexual desire as the hand of the devil.

Whether or not sex really is a route to spiritual fulfillment, it is hard to refute Brown's claim that sexual urges are natural. While no sensible person would deny that some control over them is necessary, the Christian Church went far beyond this and vilified sexuality as a whole. Its attitude can be partly explained in terms of Christian origins—the religion arose in the late Roman Empire, when sexuality had become unusually brutalized and degraded—but even so, Brown's point is not to be dismissed. The demonization of sexuality has indeed proved a potent form of social manipulation. The Jewish Law forbade sexual expression in certain circumstances, but

Christianity came close to condemning it in virtually all instances, even in marriage. As the Church Father Jerome declared, "One who loves his wife too passionately commits adultery." This would naturally produce tremendous amounts of guilt in believers—since no normal person is devoid of sexual feelings—thus enabling the Church to set itself up as the sole provider of remission of these "sins." Indeed the Church's assertion that it possesses exclusive rights to dispensing God's grace on earth—expressed in the aphorism *Extra ecclesiam nulla salus*: "outside the church there is no salvation"—is one of its bizarrest but most successful tactics.

One final issue remains. In the end, *The Da Vinci Code* states that the goal of the Priory is neither to preserve the secret of Jesus's marriage to Mary Magdalene nor to promote the interests of his bloodline. Rather, it is to foster awareness of the Divine Feminine, and, we are told, this purpose can be discerned in art, literature, even in the productions of Walt Disney. "Her story is being told in art, music, and books," Sophie's grandmother, a descendant of Christ and Mary Magdalene, tells Langdon. "Look around you. The pendulum is swinging. We are starting to sense the dangers of our history . . . and of our destructive paths. We are beginning to sense the need to restore the sacred feminine."

This states a theme that recurs in much of contemporary spiritual writing: humanity has been in bondage to masculine values of hierarchy, war, and domination for thousands of years, and now the tide is beginning to turn. The blossoming of interest in the feminine face of God—Mary Magdalene; Sophia, the personification of divine wisdom; and the Virgin herself, not to mention the Great Goddess of paganism—attests to this fact. Masculine values are receding, and we are witnessing the dawn of a new era of peace, cooperation, and caring.

There is only one problem with this vision: the contemporary scene does not bear it out. Even if we simplistically equate masculinity with domination and femininity with caring and compassion, we see less and less of the latter in society, supplanted by an ever more pervasive profit motive. In much of the developed world, the "nanny state" of the mid-twentieth century, which was intended (with whatever degree of success) to provide a level of support for all citizens, is being replaced by a laissez-faire system that assumes that market forces will somehow establish social justice.

Thus the resurgence of the Divine Feminine may represent, not a swinging of the pendulum in the other direction, but what psychologists call *compensation*. The more the virtues associated with femininity—caring, beauty, compassion—are trampled down in the culture at large, the more they will make their presence felt at an unconscious level. In individuals this manifests in dreams and neuroses, while at a collective level it manifests in spontaneous and inexplicable occurrences (such as the numerous Marian apparitions), as well as in works like *The Da Vinci Code* that seize the popular imagination. Thus these evidences of the Divine Feminine may represent, not the dawning of a brilliant new age, but a coping mechanism for the discomforts of our current situation.

Which, then, is it? Are these proclamations of the advent of the Divine Feminine simply a means that our collective mind is using to adjust itself to an uncaring and technocratic age? Or are they premonitions of a milder time to come? Certainly there is little evidence to suggest this new age is here or that its arrival is inevitable. Even so, there is one thing that leaves room for optimism. Everything in this world eventually turns into its opposite: good gives rise to evil, light to dark. And so it may happen that the coldness of our own time will reverse itself and bear fruit in an age of healing, beauty, and wisdom. If so, *The Da Vinci Code*, with all its faults, factual and literary, will have served as a harbinger of this better era.

*Five*

# 2012

THE END OF THE WORLD is a moving goalpost, or, if you prefer, the carrot on the end of an ever-receding stick that has been dangled in front of the human race for millennia now. Around A.D. 1000, when it was widely believed that Christ would come back to judge the quick and the dead, deeds were sometimes drawn up stipulating that the property transfer would be valid only until the Lord's return. Early nineteenth-century America was convulsed by the predictions of a self-taught Bible student named William Miller, who, basing his assumptions on a convoluted interpretation of Daniel and Revelation, predicted that the world would end between March 21, 1843, and March 21, 1844. Later in the century, an American haberdasher named Charles Taze Russell, making similar calculations, forecast that the end would come in 1914.

All of these prophecies failed. To these we could add

many more; indeed it sometimes seems that there is scarcely one year in the last two thousand which has not been predicted by someone, somewhere, to mark the end of time. Practically all of these (in the Western world, at any rate) were based on the more cryptic parts of the Bible. But as Christianity began to lose its exclusive hold on the religious imagination of the West, apocalyptic thought began to take inspiration from other sources.

One of these derives from the precession of the equinoxes. This phenomenon results from a slight wobble in the earth's rotation, which means that the axis is tilted slightly, approximately 23½ degrees. The axis revolves slowly over a period of slightly less than twenty-six thousand years (one figure given is 25,765 years, another, 25,920; the figure is not exact because the speed of the precession is not consistent). This means, among other things, that over the course of time the sun will rise and set in front of different constellations at different times of the year. During the last two thousand years, the sun at the March 21 equinox has had Pisces behind it. Sometime in the near future—or possibly already—the sun will have Aquarius behind it. Many in the world of esoteric thought have said that this points to a change in the ages: we will move from the Age of Pisces to the Age of Aquarius.

Exactly when this will happen is not entirely clear, for the simple reason that there is no line drawn in the sky indicating exactly where Pisces ends and Aquarius begins. I have heard opinions about the date of the transition that place it as early as 1600 and as late as 2500. Some have placed it at February 5, 1962, because there was a large stellium (cluster of planets) in Aquarius at that time: all the visible planets were in Aquarius. The choice is an interesting one: although nothing earthshaking happened on that particular day (actress Jennifer Jason Leigh was born; French president Charles de Gaulle proclaimed the independence of Algeria), 1962 was the year of the Cuban Missile Crisis—the point in history when the world has come closest to nuclear war. Moreover, this was also the onset of the 1960s, when characteristically Aquarian virtues such as innovation, individualism, unconventionality, and indeed eccentricity came to the fore on the cultural scene.

Personally, I would be tempted to place the key transition between Pisces and Aquarius slightly earlier, at the time of the two World Wars. One of the chief reasons that World War I *became* a world war was that imperial Germany under Kaiser Wilhelm II was attempting to build a navy that would rival Britain's. At the turn of the twentieth century, there was a theory prominent in political thought known as "navalism." Inspired by an American historian named Alfred Thayer Mahan, author of *The Influence of Sea Power on History, 1660–1783*, the theory held that military and political supremacy was based on *naval* supremacy: Britain's then-enormous world empire was due to its sea power. Kaiser Wilhelm, influenced by these ideas, decided that his country would vie with the British for supremacy at sea and launched an intense buildup of the German navy. The British could not stand for this. When war broke out in 1914, Britain, which ordinarily avoided involvement in wars on the European continent, joined in. The "General European War," foreseen and perhaps desired by many statesmen for years, became a World War. At much the same time, Japanese leaders were inspired by Mahan's theory to expand into the Pacific, setting the stage for conflict in World War II.

There is some reason for seeing the two World Wars as in a way continuous, even though they were interrupted by a strange and unquiet twenty-year interregnum. Certainly World War II pitted largely the same powers against each other as had its predecessor. But the outcome of World War II was not decided by sea power (although Allied supremacy at sea in both the Atlantic and Pacific was a necessary condition for success). It was decided by air. The audacious Allied invasion of Europe in 1944 succeeded only because the Allies by then had overwhelming supremacy in the air. And of course the war ended when the United States dropped atomic bombs on Hiroshima and Nagasaki in August 1945—again from the air. The World Wars began because of sea power but were won by air power.

Astrologically, Pisces is a water sign, Aquarius an air sign. Could these large-scale historical trends mean that on a global level we have moved from an age of water to one of air? In this case, the Age of Aquarius might be said to have begun in 1903, with the flight of the Wright brothers' first airplane.

But neither 1903 nor 1914 nor 1945 is cited very often as the dawning of the Age of Aquarius. In the twentieth century, some were pointing toward a date around the turn of the millennium. The Swiss psychologist C. G. Jung, writing in 1951, said:

> Astrologically the beginning of the next aeon, according to the starting point you select, falls between A.D. 2000 and 2200. Starting from star 'O' [in Pisces] and assuming a Platonic month of 2,143 years, one would arrive at A.D. 2154 for the beginning of the Aquarian Age, and at A.D. 1997 if you start from star 'a 113.' The latter date agrees with the longitude of the stars in Ptolemy's Almagest.

Since Ptolemy is one of the greatest astrological authorities of all time, Jung would seem to be hinting that he himself preferred 1997. This date would jibe with prophecies coming from quite another source: the Mayan calendar as analyzed by archaeoastronomers. John Major Jenkins, author of *Mayan Cosmogenesis 2012*, says that the Mayan calendar, with its numerous and almost incomprehensible reckonings of cycles within cycles (including a "Long Count" spanning 1,872,000 days or some 5,129 years), points to a key juncture: the time when the point of the December solstice aligns precisely with the center of the galaxy. "The precise alignment of the solstice point (the precise center-point of the body of the sun as viewed from earth) with the Galactic equator was calculated to occur in 1998," Jenkins observes on his Web site, www.alignment2012.com. Because it takes about thirty-six years for the solstice point to move through this equator, Major says, "the Galactic Alignment 'zone' is 1998 +/− 18 years = 1980–2016. This is 'era-2012.' This Galactic Alignment occurs only once every 26,000 years, and was what the ancient Maya were pointing to with the 2012 end-date of their Long Count calendar."

Why are so many arrows pointing to 2012? The answer can be stated fairly simply. December 21, 2012, is the end of the current Long Cycle of the Mayan calendar that began over 5,100 years ago. But this does not tell us why this obscure and intricate calendar from a lost civilization should interest us today.

The concept of 2012 as a crux in human history owes its popularity to the late José Argüelles, author of a number of books including *The Mayan Factor*. Argüelles is best known as the chief herald of the Harmonic Convergence of 1987, an event in which millions of people received—or attempted to receive—galactic energies that, Argüelles contended, were streaming to the earth and awakening a higher consciousness. But 1987 was only a prelude. The key date, said Argüelles, is 2012—specifically December 21, 2012, the end of the Mayan Long Count.

Why should we pay any attention to the Mayan calendar? Although it is an intricate and ingenious attempt to coordinate the cycles of several heavenly bodies—notably the sun, the moon, and Venus—it is far from the only calendar known to humanity, and there are few if any others in which this date stands out. Argüelles's view is that the Mayan calendar, using what he calls "the 13:20 timing frequency," represents a more natural and universal series of cycles than the Western calendar. One of the reasons our civilization is out of whack, according to Argüelles, is that we are using the wrong calendar. We are moving according to an unnatural rhythm; our civilization is like a musical instrument that has been tuned to the wrong pitch. We should be basing our calendar on a thirteen-moon cycle of twenty-eight days each, as the Mayans did. (This gives us 364 days; another intercalary day would have to be added "for renewal before the new year.") According to the Thirteen Moons Web site, which promotes Argüelles's ideas, "modern humanity is in trouble because it is immersed in an erroneous and artificial perception of time which causes it to deviate at an accelerated rate from the natural order of the universe. To remedy this situation, Argüelles has been promoting the return to a natural timing cycle through the regular measure of the Thirteen Moon 28-day calendar."

Argüelles and Jenkins are not the only visionaries to point to 2012. The late Terence McKenna, who served as a kind of psychedelic guru to the generation that came of age in the 1980s and '90s, reached a similar conclusion. In his book *The Invisible Landscape*, McKenna described a mathematical function that he called a "timewave." It was meant to mark what the British philosopher Alfred North Whitehead called the "ingression of novelty" into the world: that is, peaks in human insight and creativity. McKenna's timewave has peaks and troughs throughout history. One of these peaks came in the late 1960s. Because the wave shortens as history progresses, each "ingression" happens sixty-four times faster than its predecessor. The next peak was due in 2010; after that, the peaks increase in frequency from years to months to days until the wave compresses to zero. McKenna calculated that this point would come on December 22, 2012—astonishingly close to the date of the Mayan calendar, although McKenna was apparently not aware of this coincidence when he developed his theory.

Another researcher, Carl Johan Calleman, author of *The Mayan Calendar and the Transformation of Consciousness,* who also argued that the rate of change will accelerate, pushed the date back a year, to late October 2011. "It will simply not be possible not to be enlightened after October 28, 2011," he proclaims, "or at least from a certain time afterward when the new reality has definitely manifested." But as of this writing in April 2012, the new reality has definitely *not* manifested.

Even from this brief discussion, some themes are starting to stand out. One is the premonition of some kind of apocalyptic change—but a change in consciousness, not the result of divine apparitions. While apocalyptic shifts in everything from the global climate to the earth's magnetic field are frequently cited, it is really a change of mind or heart that many of these visionaries are stressing. Daniel Pinchbeck writes in his book *2012: The Return of Quetzalcoatl*:

> I have proposed that this intensifying global crisis is the material expression of a psycho-spiritual process, forcing our transition to a new and more intensified state of awareness. If Calleman's hypothesis is correct, this telescoping of time will mean a high-speed replay of aspects of past historical epochs—echoes of the French Revolution, the rise and fall of the Third Reich, and so on—before consciousness reaches the next twist of the spiral.

As part of this transition, we will reintegrate the aboriginal and mythic worldviews, recognizing the essential importance of spiritual evolution, while understanding that this evolution is directly founded upon our relationship to material and physical aspects of reality. The higher conscious-ness and conscience of our species will be forged through the process of putting the broken and intri-cate shards of our world back together, piece by piece.

For all this, 2012 is a somewhat softer date than is often proclaimed. It does seem to be the case that the Mayan Long Cycle ends on the December solstice of that year, but as Jenkins points out, this is merely part of a much longer process that spans thirty-six years, most of which have passed already. Jenkins places the peak of this era at 1998. Calleman says it is actually 2011. As for the coming of the Aquarian Age, there is simply no agreement among astrologers.

We thus find ourselves in the customary situation with prophecy: elaborate calculations, forecasts of doom and redemption, thrills of hope and shudders of despair, along with some fuzziness about the details. It is amusing and instructive to see that these prophecies are mirror images of fundamentalist Christian predictions of the End Times, even though the two camps hold each other in more or less complete detestation.

In short, it would be extremely difficult to base any serious expectations for the future on the 2012 date. Of course at this writing I can't say that *nothing* will happen; that would be making a prophecy as much as if I were to say that it will. But at the very least one can be forgiven if one fails to take 2012 terribly seriously as a marker for Armageddon, mass enlightenment, or anything else.

All the same, it is not quite so simple. As with so many things pertaining to the occult or the paranormal, one senses that one is stepping into a shifting, liminal area. Things are seen, but only out of the corner of one's eye. No sooner does one embrace an apparent fact than the evidence for it seems to vanish from one's hands. No sooner does one dismiss a phenomenon as absurd or irrational than something tugs at the sleeve to suggest that it may not be so absurd after all.

Take, for example, what are commonly called "earth changes"—the belief that cataclysmic shifts in the natural world are about to descend on us. A few decades ago, these were the province of figures like Edgar Cayce (1877–1945), the "sleeping prophet" who foresaw that various parts of the world would sink into the ocean. Here is the most famous of his earth changes prophecies, from a reading he gave in 1934:

The earth will be broken up in the western portion of America. The greater portion of Japan must go into the sea. The upper portion of Europe will be changed as in the twinkling of an eye. Land will appear off the east coast of America. There will be the upheavals in the Arctic and in the Antarctic that will make for the eruption of volcanos in the Torrid areas, and there will be shifting then of the poles— so that where there has been those of a frigid or the semi-tropical will become the more tropical, and moss and fern will grow. And these will begin in those periods in '58 to '98, when these will be proclaimed as the periods when His light will be seen again in the clouds. As to times, as to seasons, as to places, ALONE is it given to those who have named the name—and who bear the mark of those of His calling and His election in their bodies. To them it shall be given.

Not so long ago, these predictions would have sounded ridiculous to anyone who was not a believer. They do not sound quite so ridiculous now. Several years ago I received a newsletter from my representative to the U.S. Congress. It contained a map that outlined what parts of the world were due to be submerged if the entire Arctic ice cap were melted (which is entirely possible; in the summer of 2007, a portion of the ice cap melted that was the size of California). The map bore more than a passing resemblance to those of earth changes that I remember being put out in the 1960s and '70s, or for that matter to the "Future Map of the World" produced by psychic Gordon-Michael Scallion. What's going on when predictions from as humdrum a source as a newsletter from a U.S. congressman (one who, moreover, used to be a chemistry professor) resemble those of the wildest visionaries?

I myself have no answers; my own explorations in the realm of prophecy haven't proved sound enough for me to suggest anything on my own. But it does seem that we are in a time analogous to the Belle Époque ("beautiful era"), a name given to the period of European history from 1890 to 1914. It was an age when civilization appeared to have reached its peak and when the European nations that ruled most of the earth's surface congratulated themselves on their own superiority. And yet under the surface lay disorder and discontent, evidenced in revolts, uprisings, assassinations of statesmen. What followed—the World Wars, with all their attendant horrors—proved that the growing awareness of moral and intellectual bankruptcy of the world's leadership during the Belle Époque had been all too accurate.

We have reached a similar turn in the spiral. Our technological developments have outstripped our moral development. Our political leaders continue to play the old game of mass manipulation for the advantage of the wealthy and powerful when it is their duty to protect their people from what U.S. President Theodore Roosevelt called "the malefactors of great wealth." The earth changes—now reported by science rather than prophesied by occultists—are both pressingly obvious and largely ignored by those with the power to do anything about them.

The solution seems clear. In one way or another, all the heralds of 2012 that we've looked at here have pointed to it: we need to make a leap of consciousness. And yet in a way this is missing the point. What we are lacking, in the strict sense, is not consciousness. We know what the problems are; we know what would solve them; even in a narrowly technical sense, many of the solutions are ready to hand. But we have not had the strength or the will to implement them. The world has been more than happy to go on with business as usual much as it always has—offering lip service to its ideals while traducing them in practice.

If there is any truth to the 2012 prophecies, all this will have to change. We will either adopt or be forced to adopt some entirely new ways of behaving that are not so new. After all, if everyone simply decided to live by the ethical ideals that we all know to be right, many and indeed most of the world's problems would vanish as if by magic. Whether that will happen is hard to say. Human nature has proved to be by far the most stubborn and resistant of all the obstacles we have had to face.

On the other hand, for all the upheavals, inner and outer, that may confront us in times to come—and we do not know what they will be, for all the prophecies—it seems certain that the fundamental issues and experiences of human life will remain the same. And the work we must do on ourselves will remain the same. The Buddha reminded us of these truths in his dying words: "Now, monks, this I say to you: Transient are all created things. Work out your salvation with diligence."

### SOURCES

Howell, Alice O. *The Heavens Declare: Astrological Ages and the Evolution of Consciousness.* Wheaton, Ill.: Quest Books, 2006.

Hughes, Amy, ed. *The Mystery of 2012: Predictions, Prophecies, and Possibilities.* Boulder, Colo.: Sounds True, 2007.

Jung, C. G. *Aion: Researches into the Phenomenology of the Self.* Translated by R. F. C. Hull. 2nd ed. Princeton, N.J.: Princeton/Bollingen, 1959.

Pinchbeck, Daniel. *2012: The Return of Quetzalcoatl.* New York: Tarcher/Penguin, 2006.

*Six*

# RENÉ GUÉNON AND
# THE KALI YUGA

CURRENTLY THE FEAR—OR HOPE—of the closing of
the age pervades the air like a thick vapor. Sometimes
this end is envisaged as an environmental calamity, sometimes as the second coming of Christ, sometimes as the
return of the space brothers to claim their own. Figures
including Jose Argüelles, the prophet of the 1987 Harmonic Convergence; Terence McKenna, the late pope of
psychedelia; and the channeled entity known as Kryon
have fastened onto 2012 as the turning point. A less well
known, though in a way equally influential, figure was the
French esoteric philosopher René Guénon, whose writings
often speak of the end of a cycle that he equated with the
Kali Yuga, the "dark age" of Hindu cosmology. While he
did not point to 2012 or any other specific date, his ideas do
resonate with some of these expectations for the dawning
age to come.

Born in Blois, France, in 1886, Guénon had a conventional education in mathematics. In his youth he began to explore occult currents in Paris and was initiated into esoteric groups connected with Freemasonry, Martinism, Taoism, and Advaita Vedanta. In 1911, he was initiated into a Sufi *tariqah* (order) under the leadership of an Egyptian sheikh, Abder Rahman Elish El-Kebir. In 1930, he moved to Egypt, where he converted to Islam and lived until his death in 1951. In the meantime, he published a wide range of books, articles, and reviews espousing what he said was the universal and primordial tradition underlying all religions.

For Guénon, tradition is the *ne plus ultra* of human life. He conceives of tradition as a hierarchy: higher knowledge emanates from a now-hidden spiritual center to all of humankind through the "orthodox" traditions, among which he includes (with many caveats and qualifications) the great world religions as well as certain other lines such as Freemasonry. Or to put it more accurately, this tradition is preserved in certain initiatic lineages that lie embedded in these faiths, such as the Kabbalah in Judaism, Taoism in Chinese religion, and Sufism in Islam. The esoteric dimension of Christianity had, he believed, practically disappeared by the late Middle Ages and was now preserved (if at all) by small initiatic groups that he apparently regarded as inaccessible. Indeed Guénon's conversion to Islam was motivated in part by his belief that these Western lineages had almost completely died out by the twentieth century.

In fact, according to Guénon, this transmission of traditional knowledge—the "doctrine," as he often styles it—has become almost completely blocked in our era. This, he argued, is the result of a long cosmic cycle, which is called a "Manvantara" in Hindu cosmology, and which is divided into four *yugas* or ages: the Satya Yuga, the Treta Yuga, the Dvapara Yuga, and the present Kali Yuga. The problems and anxieties of the current era are the result of this age. It's worth exploring why he believed this and what he thought it meant.

Guénon was first and foremost a metaphysician—indeed, he was one of the greatest and most lucid thinkers who have delved into this arcane subject. And for him, metaphysics concerns universal principles; the details of circumstance are of value only insofar as they illustrate these. At the beginning of his best-known work, *The Reign of Quantity and the Signs of the Times* (first published in 1945), he writes that "considerations of that order"—namely, factual details—"are worth nothing except in so far as they represent an application of principles to certain particular circumstances."[1]

---

[1]René Guénon, *The Reign of Quantity and the Signs of the Times*, trans. Lord Northbourne (Harmondsworth, Middlesex, U.K.: Penguin, 1972), 7.

Guénon was not a prophet in any conventional sense. He was not a visionary and believed that the visionary prophecy of the current age was nothing more than a cloud of lies emitted by sinister "counterinitiatic" forces. If he spoke of an outlook that made it possible "to foresee, at least in its broad outlines, what will be the shape of a future world," he insisted that "previsions of this kind have not really any 'divinatory' character whatever, but are founded entirely on . . . the qualitative determinations of time."[2]

The use of the word "qualitative" may seem peculiar here, but for Guénon, the polarity between "quality" and "quantity" was central to understanding the dynamics at play. In his 1931 book *The Symbolism of the Cross*, he depicted reality in the form of a three-dimensional cross—one that has the dimension of height and depth in addition to the familiar two of length and breadth. At the top of this cross is what he called "absolute quality"—an abstract state that is impossible for us to conceive, because it has no element of quantity whatsoever. (An interesting mind game: try to conceive of a universe in which there is no number or quantity of any sort. It's almost impossible to do.) At the bottom of this cross is "absolute quantity"—another abstract state that is impossible to conceive. (Again, try to imagine a universe where there is *only* number, in which

---

[2] Guénon, *The Reign of Quantity*, 57.

there is nothing that has any particular qualities such as color, shape, or anything else of the kind.)

Hence it's not possible in this relative level of existence to reach the absolute end of each pole, but in a given age, one of the two will be more pronounced and the other less pronounced to an exactly inverse degree. According to Guénon, the Manvantara proceeds in an ages-long cycle from an era where quality is emphasized—the legendary time known to the Hindus as the Satya Yuga and to the ancient Greeks as the Golden Age—to one in which quantity comes more and more to dominate. This is our present era, the Kali Yuga or what the Greeks called the Iron Age. That's why Guénon speaks of the present era as one of "the reign of quantity." He goes on to argue that all the primary characteristics of our time are the result of this reign of quantity.

Guénon produces modern philosophy and science as evidence for his argument. Modern Western philosophy to all intents and purposes begins with René Descartes (1596–1650), who divided the world into what he called *res cogitans* (literally, "the thing that thinks") and *res extensa* (literally, "the extended thing"). That is to say, the world is divided into that which *experiences*—*res cogitans*—and that which *is experienced*: *res extensa*. According to Descartes (at least as interpreted by Guénon), everything material is characterized by—and *only* by—extension, by what can be measured and quantified.

While this all may sound extremely abstract, Guénon argued—rightly, I believe—that this attitude has profoundly shaped Western thought over the last few centuries. Essentially, he is saying, materialistic science focuses exclusively on quantity: "The more specifically 'scientific' point of view as the modern world understands it . . . seeks to bring everything down to quantity, anything that cannot be so treated is not taken into account, and is regarded as more or less non-existent."[3] Unfortunately, as Guénon goes on to say, this creates any number of logical contradictions. Science conceived purely in terms of quantity argues that the same causes produce the same effects, but as Guénon points out, this is absurd, as no two events are ever completely identical. He also criticizes "the delusion which consists in thinking of a large number of facts can be of use in itself as 'proof' of a theory; . . . even a little thought will make it evident that facts of the same kind are always indefinite in multitude, so that they can never all be taken into account."[4]

This is precisely the problem that contemporary philosophers call "the justification of induction." You base a theory on any number of similar events that have happened in the past; but how can you account for the ones

---

[3] Guénon, *The Reign of Quantity*, 85.
[4] Guénon, *The Reign of Quantity*, 87.

that you have not seen, and how can you be sure that future facts will yield the same results? Bertrand Russell put the point wittily when he wrote, "The man who has fed the chicken every day throughout its life at last wrings its neck instead, showing that more refined views as to the uniformity of nature would have been useful to the chicken."[5] The notion of causation is at least as problematic.[6] These facts place a ceiling on the degree to which science can understand and explain the universe.

As even this short discussion suggests, Guénon raises profound philosophical issues, and contemporary thought has not done a terribly impressive job of coping with them. But, he contends, the problems go further still. In a chapter of *The Reign of Quantity* entitled "The Degeneration of Coinage," he explores the economic aspects of the issue. At first glance, one might think that nothing was more purely quantitative than money. But that, Guénon argues, is an illusion fostered by the degenerate age we live in: "The 'economic' point of view . . . , and the exclusively quantitative conception of money which is inherent in it, are but the products of a degeneration which is on the whole fairly recent, . . . money possessed at its origin, and retained for a

---

[5] Bertrand Russell, *The Problems of Philosophy* (New York: Barnes & Noble, 2002 [1912]), 42.
[6] For a more complete discussion of these issues, see my book *The Dice Game of Shiva: How Consciousness Creates the Universe* (Novato, Calif.: New World Library, 2009), chs. 4 and 5.

long time, quite a different character and a truly qualitative value, remarkable as this may appear to the majority of our contemporaries."[7]

In traditional societies, Guénon says, money had a sacred character. Not only were the coins stamped with the images of gods and other sacred symbols, but the currency was controlled by the spiritual authorities rather than by the secular powers. Money was meant to be a reminder of "value" in the qualitative as well as the quantitative sense. Today, however, "nobody is able any longer to conceive that money can represent anything other than a simple quantity."[8] Even such words as "value" and "estimate" have been deprived of their qualitative character, and today, when we ask how much a man is worth, we are almost always thinking in terms of cash and equities rather than moral or spiritual caliber.

This quantitative approach extends to every object we use. "In a traditional civilization," Guénon writes, "each object was at the same time as perfectly fitted as possible for the use for which it was immediately destined and also made so that it could at any moment, and owing to the very fact that real use was being made of it (instead of its being treated more or less as a dead thing as the moderns

---

[7] Guénon, *The Reign of Quantity*, 133.
[8] Guénon, *The Reign of Quantity*, 136.

do with everything that they consider to be a 'work of art'), serve as a 'support' for meditation, . . . thus helping everyone to elevate himself to a superior state according to the measure of his capacities."[9] One obvious example are the tools of Masonry, such as the square, compass, and plumb line, each of which was intended to convey a spiritual and ethical meaning in the days when Masonry was limited to practicing stonemasons. Manufactured goods have no such meaning or value.

It is not possible here to go further into Guénon's critique, but even this short discussion reveals that his insights into the woes of the current era were remarkably perceptive and prescient. In *The Crisis of the Modern World*, published in 1927, he said, "It is . . . to be expected that discoveries, or rather mechanical and industrial inventions, will go on developing and multiplying more and more rapidly until the end of the present age; and who knows if, given the dangers of destruction they bear in themselves, they will not be one of the chief agents in the ultimate catastrophe, if things reach a point at which this cannot be averted?"[10]

---

[9] Guénon, *The Reign of Quantity*, 137.

[10] René Guénon, *The Crisis of the Modern World*, trans. Arthur Osborne et al. (Ghent, N.Y.: Sophia Perennis et Universalis, 1996), 39.

Guénon's charge that the modern world has no use for anything apart from quantity could be substantiated by cases from every conceivable source. Reporting on the BP oil spill in the Gulf of Mexico, in early July 2010 a front-page article in *The Wall Street Journal* stated, "BP PLC is pushing to fix its runaway Gulf oil well by July 27, possibly weeks before the deadline the company is discussing publicly, in a bid to show investors it has capped its ballooning financial liabilities." Why did BP choose this date? "The July 27 target date is the day the company is expected to report second-quarter earnings and speak to investors."[11] In other words, the fact that the BP spill, one of the greatest environmental disasters in history, fouled a large portion of the Gulf of Mexico, killed innumerable creatures, and devastated the lives of people all along the Gulf Coast was not reason enough for the company to hurry: it needed a second-quarter earnings report to goad itself into action. Nothing could illustrate the reign of quantity more clearly.

All this said, when it comes to Guénon's discussion of the Kali Yuga as a traditional Hindu doctrine, he stands on much shakier ground. He says that the Kali Yuga began some six thousand years ago.[12] He also says this era is close

---

[11]Monica Langley, "BP Sets New Spill Target," *The Wall Street Journal*, July 8, 2010, A1.

[12]René Guénon, *The King of the World*, trans. Henry D. Fohr (Hillsdale, N.Y.: Sophia Perennis et Universalis, 2001), 49.

to its end. In *The Crisis of the Modern World*, he writes: "We have in fact entered upon the last phase of the Kali-Yuga, the darkest period of the 'dark age,' the state of dissolution from which it is impossible to emerge otherwise than by a cataclysm."[13]

Not all traditional sources agree about this point. The Hindu sage Sri Yukteswar, best known as the master of the celebrated yogi Paramahansa Yogananda, discusses the matter in his book *The Holy Science*. Sri Yukteswar says that the Kali Yuga is actually over, although this has not been recognized even by many Hindu authorities. Ironically in light of Guénon's claims, it was the very occlusion of the sacred center that made it impossible to calculate the yugas correctly.

Traditional dating for the beginning of the Kali Yuga starts from the death of Krishna, the avatar of Vishnu, at the end of the war between the Pandava and Kaurava clans chronicled in the Hindu epic the *Mahabharata*. Some sources date this to 3012 B.C., others to 1400 B.C.[14] As the Kali Yuga began to dawn, Yudhisthira—the victorious Pandava king—gave his throne over to his grandson, Raja Parikshit. "Together with all the wise men of his court," according to Sri Yukteswar, Yudhisthira "retired to the

---

[13]Guénon, *The Crisis of the Modern World*, 17.
[14]See Klaus R. Kostermaier, *A Survey of Hinduism*, 3d ed. (Albany: State University of New York Press, 2007), 97.

Himalayan Mountains, the paradise of the world. Thus there was none in the court of Raja Parikshit who could understand the principle of correctly calculating the ages of the several Yugas."[15]

Sri Yukteswar maintains that the Kali Yuga actually ended in A.D. 1699. While his views may have been imbued with a belief in progress by his own British education and do not necessarily correspond with those of the majority of Hindus, at any rate his claim to being a source of "traditional" knowledge is much higher than Guénon's. David Frawley, an American Vedic astrologer, agrees with Sri Yukteswar in saying that the Kali Yuga ended in 1699.[16] In any event, the dating is far from clear-cut. In fact many traditional sources reckon on a much larger scale for the duration of the Kali Yuga, placing its length at 432,000 years. If this were the case, it would render any imminent end to this epoch highly improbable.[17]

One of the sources that come closest to Guénon's view of the Kali Yuga is H. P. Blavatsky (1831–1891), founder of the Theosophical Society. In her magnum opus, *The Secret*

[15]Jnananavatar Swami Sri Yukteswar, *The Holy Science* (Los Angeles: Self-Realization Fellowship, 1990), 16–17.

[16]David Frawley, *Astrology of the Seers: A Guide to Vedic/Hindu Astrology* (Twin Lakes, Wis.: Lotus, 2000), 36–39.

[17]For a helpful summary of the various views, see Joseph Morales, "The Hindu Theory of World Cycles in the Light of Modern Science": http://baharna .com/karma/yuga.htm; accessed January 14, 2010.

*Doctrine*, Blavatsky writes, "The Kali-yuga reigns now supreme in India, and it seems to coincide with the Western age."[18] Blavatsky, writing around 1888, dates the beginning of this epoch to "4,989 years ago"—close to the traditional date of 3012 B.C.—and places its end roughly at the close of the nineteenth century: "We have not long to wait, and many of us will witness the Dawn of the New Cycle."[19]

This resemblance is peculiar, because Guénon loathed Blavatsky and Theosophy and criticized them in his first published book, *Theosophy: History of a Pseudo-Religion*. For Guénon, Theosophy was the ultimate counterinitiatic force, distorting and perverting the truth of traditional knowledge. He especially detested the Theosophical doctrine of evolution, which teaches that each living thing—indeed each atom—is progressing on a cycle of devolution into matter followed by evolution into higher consciousness. The Theosophical view is similar to Guénon's in saying that the present era is the one in which materiality is most dominant and that it is coming to an end, but it generally portrays the progress of the human race in far more positive terms than Guénon.

The connections between Guénon and Theosophy are intricate. One of his first spiritual teachers was the occult-

---

[18]H. P. Blavatsky, *The Secret Doctrine* (Wheaton, Ill.: Quest, 1993 [1888]), 1:377.
[19]Blavatsky, *Secret Doctrine*, 1:xliii–xliv.

ist Papus (Gérard Encausse), who was head of the French branch of the Theosophical Society, and the scholar Mark Sedgwick, whose book *Against the Modern World* is the best introduction to the impact of Guénon's thought, sees Theosophy as one of Guénon's chief influences.[20] While it is impossible to go into this controversy here, it is at least clear that both Blavatsky and Guénon believed the end of the Kali Yuga was at hand. Another central figure in the esotericism of the twentieth century, C. G. Jung, did not deal at length with the Kali Yuga, but in *Aion*, his compendious analysis of the symbolism of the astrological ages, he suggests 1997 as the starting point of the New Age, for intricate astronomical reasons.[21]

Are we, then, at the end of a cycle? In one sense, yes, of course we are. There are many cycles in nature: every year, every day, is the end of a cycle. But whether we are at the end of the Kali Yuga is, at the very least, moot. My own impression is that the more genuinely traditional Hindus tend to see the Kali Yuga in terms of the much longer time frame of 432,000 years. While Guénon reviled the West and its attempt to erode the traditional values of Asian civilization, ironically his view that the end is at hand

[20]Mark Sedgwick, *Against the Modern World: Traditionalism and the Secret Intellectual History of the Twentieth Century* (Oxford: Oxford University Press, 2004), 40–44.
[21]C. G. Jung, *Aion: Researches into the Phenomenology of the Self*, trans. R. F. C. Hull (Princeton, N.J.: Princeton/Bollingen, 1959), 94.

comes far closer to the spirit of Christianity, the ultimate Western religion—which for two thousand years has been predicting the imminent return of Jesus—than it does to Hindu thought.

What does this mean in practical terms for us today? Waiting for the end of the world (or of the age) is a kind of narcotic. It enables the human mind to accommodate its own notion of cosmic justice to the realities at hand (because the wicked—who are always, of course, the *others*—will be brought low, while the good—oneself and whatever group one identifies with—will be exalted). It also serves as what psychology calls a displacement of the fear of death. For each of us individually, the end of the world is certainly coming, in a few decades at the very longest. But human beings dislike contemplating the certainty of death. They find it easier to deal with by casting it in the remote and highly improbable form of whatever cataclysm happens to suit the fashions of the moment. (For a fuller treatment of this dynamic, see the chapter "Nostradamus and the Uses of Prophecy" in my book *The Essential Nostradamus*.)

Unfortunately, we cannot stand around waiting for the end of the world to solve our problems for us. If we genuinely are at a threshold of a new era, we will be able to cross it only if we discard the contrived apocalypticism that suffuses mass culture and to which Guénon, as powerful a thinker as he was, was not immune.

Nevertheless, Guénon's claim that we are living under the reign of quantity is hard to refute. One has only to read prominent periodicals such as *The Wall Street Journal* and *The Economist* to see that the real protagonist in all their stories is money—money in the abstract, as a kind of hypostatized entity that stipulates all value and dictates all morality. What is good, we are told, is what is good for money. Whether or not the Kali Yuga is about to end, we can bring the end of the reign of quantity a few steps closer by looking into ourselves and making sure that the values by which we guide our lives are more than merely economic ones.

# Seven

# ATLANTIS THEN
# AND NOW

To this day Atlantis haunts the psyche of humankind. A half-forgotten continent that sank overnight into the ocean, reputed to have been the secret source of civilizations as far-flung as those of Egypt and Central America, it is believed to have had wondrous technology, natural and supernatural, and to have attained a level of development that we have yet to match. Even though no one has ever found any unassailable material evidence of this civilization, there are few ideas that reappear as often in occult literature.

Skeptics continue to jeer at the notion of a lost continent, but such a thing does not seem as unbelievable as it may once have—certainly not, for example, to the inhabitants of Malé, the island capital of the Republic of the Maldives in the Indian Ocean, threatened with submersion as global warming continues to raise sea levels. Once we admit this possibility, we may find ourselves asking whether the fall of Atlantis could be repeated with our own civilization, vexed as it is with fears of ecodisaster.

The legend of Atlantis first appears in two dialogues by the Greek philosopher Plato (c. 427–347 B.C.)—the *Timaeus* and the *Critias*. These texts have been cornerstones of the Western esoteric tradition for millennia, and not because of their discussion of Atlantis: the *Timaeus* in particular describes a cosmology that would leave its impact on mystical traditions ranging from Gnosticism and Hermeticism to the Kabbalah. But it is the story of Atlantis that has most captured the public imagination.

Before we go into this account, it's necessary to point out that many of Plato's dialogues contain myths. They are not the traditional myths of Greek religion but compositions of his own. One of the most famous examples is found at the end of *The Republic*. It describes a near-death experience of a soldier named Er, who goes to the realm of Hades and returns, telling of the Homeric heroes who drew lots for the lives they would lead in the next incarnation. While Plato no doubt believed in reincarnation, this story has obviously been made up to fit its setting. Many scholars regard the tale of Atlantis as a myth in this sense, even though Critias, the narrator of this account, insists that it is "a tale, which, though strange, is certainly true, having been attested by Solon, who was the wisest of the seven sages" (*Timaeus* 20d–e).[1] Critias's testimony in this dialogue has a ring of truth, because Solon—a lawmaker and poet who lived c. 600 B.C. and who, as we have seen, was renowned for his wisdom—was a relative of one of Critias's ancestors. Plato himself belonged to the same clan; hence the story of Atlantis could have been a family tradition that Plato knew firsthand.

Critias's story, which in fact revolves around Athens, is placed nine thousand years before Solon's time—that is, around 9600 B.C. We learn that Solon in turn heard it from an Egyptian priest, who told him, "there have been, and there will be again, many destructions of mankind arising out of many causes; the greatest have been brought about by fire and water." The priest adds, "you remember a single deluge only"—the Greeks had a legend of a flood like the one in the Bible—"but there were many previous ones" (*Timaeus* 22c, 23b).

Before this flood, the priest goes on to say, there was an enormous island called Atlantis, "situated in front of the straits which are by you called the Pillars of Heracles [the

---

[1]Quotations from the *Timaeus* are taken from Benjamin Jowett's translation in Edith Hamilton and Huntington Cairns, eds., *Plato: The Collected Dialogues* (Princeton, N.J.: Princeton/Bollingen, 1961); the quotation from the *Critias* is from A. E. Taylor's translation in the same edition.

strait of Gibraltar]. The island was larger than Libya[2] and Asia put together, and was the way to other islands, and from these you might pass to the whole of the opposite continent which surrounded the true ocean" (*Timaeus* 25e).

The empire of Atlantis "had subjected the parts of Libya within the columns of Heracles as far as Egypt, and of Europe as far as Tyrrhenia [modern-day Italy]," and was moving to subjugate Egypt and Greece as well. It was then, according to the Egyptian priest, that Athens resisted the Atlantean invaders.

> After having undergone the very extremity of danger, she defeated and triumphed over the invaders, and preserved from slavery those who were not yet subjugated, and generously liberated all the rest of us who dwell within the Pillars. But afterward there occurred violent earthquakes and floods, and in a single day and night of misfortune all your warlike men in a body sank into the earth, and the island of Atlantis in like manner disappeared in the depths of the sea. For which reason the sea in those parts is impassable and impenetrable, because there is a shoal of mud in the way, and this was caused by the subsidence of the island." (*Timaeus* 25c–d)

---

[2]The ancient Greeks sometimes referred to the continent of Africa as "Libya."

The same inundation swept Greece as well, stripping its soil and leaving it comparatively barren, as it was in Plato's time and still is today.

How literally did Plato mean his readers to take this myth? Like nearly all of his surviving work, the *Timaeus* is in the form of a dialogue, a genre that allows the author to stand back a step from the assertions in it: they are not necessarily Plato's claims but those of the people he is quoting. Nevertheless, Crantor, the earliest commentator on the *Timaeus*, writing around 300 B.C., accepted it as genuine history, as did the ancient authorities Strabo and Posidonius.[3]

Plato's date of 9600 B.C. is intriguingly close to the end of the last glacial period on earth—around 10,000 B.C.—at which time some land that was above water was submerged (e.g., the continental shelf that had formed a land bridge between Britain and mainland Europe), so the disappearance of the fabled land fits reasonably well into conventional scientific chronology. Nonetheless, it is still necessary to find a plausible site for the lost continent. For some bizarre reason, the most popular choice has been Thera (present-day Santorini), an island in the Mediterranean much of whose land mass was destroyed in a cataclysmic

---

[3]"Atlantis," Wikipedia: http://en.wikipedia.org/wiki/Atlantis; accessed Jan. 12, 2011. Cf. "Atlantis," in Simon Hornblower and Anthony Spawforth, eds., *The Oxford Classical Dictionary*, 3d ed. (Oxford: Oxford University Press, 1996).

eruption of a volcano sometime between 1650 and 1500 B.C. But since Thera does not match Plato's Atlantis in location or size (Thera is in the Mediterranean and is much smaller) and since the date of the eruption is nowhere near Plato's estimate, it is an unlikely host for the doomed civilization.

The most plausible candidate for Atlantis is an obscure geological formation known as the Horseshoe Seamount Chain, located in the Atlantic about six hundred kilometers west of Gibraltar. This is a series of nine inactive volcanoes, which rise from an abyssal plain of 4,000 to 4,800 meters deep. The highest, the Ampère Seamount, nearly reaches the sea surface. Thus, in the last Ice Age, it could conceivably have been above sea level. The area in the Atlantic is also a meeting place for three major oceanic flow systems, making its currents unusually disturbed.[4] The horseshoe shape of the formation also evokes Plato's description of Atlantis, whose inhabitants "bridged the rings of sea round their original home" (*Critias*, 115c).

After Atlantis sank, according to Plato, the area beyond Gibraltar was impossible to navigate because of the mud shoals. Aristotle, in his *Meteorologica*, also mentions "shallows due to mud" in this area, and another ancient

---

[4] Jörn Hatzky, "Physiography of the Ampère Seamount in the Horseshoe Seamount Chain off Gibraltar," Alfred Wegener Institute for Polar and Marine Research, Bremerhaven (2005): http://doi.pangaea.de/10.1594/PANGAEA.341125; accessed Jan. 12, 2011.

source, Scylax of Caryanda, mentions a sea of thick mud just beyond the Pillars of Hercules. The Web site "Return to Atlantis" observes, "It seems that even as recently as 2,300 years ago—which on the geological scale is barely an eye-blink—the Ocean beyond Gibraltar was unnavigable because of deposits of mud from a vanished island. Even today an examination of the sea bed at this point reveals an exceptionally high level of sedimentation."[5]

The only difference between this site and Plato's Atlantis is that the latter was a continent larger than Asia and Africa put together. While this is implausible, Plato also says that Atlantis "was the way to other islands, and from these you might pass to the whole of the opposite continent which surrounded the true ocean, for this sea which is within the Straits of Heracles [i.e., the Mediterranean] is only a harbor, having a narrow entrance, but that other is a real sea, and the land surrounding it on every side may be most truly called a boundless continent" (*Timaeus* 25a).

This remarkable passage suggests that—contrary to the usual beliefs—the ancients knew that there was a continent across the Atlantic, to which Atlantis once served as a gateway. Although the Americas do not surround the Atlantic, they can, from an ancient point of view, be termed

---

5 http://www.returntoatlantis.com/retc/gradual.html; accessed Jan. 12, 2011. Cf. Aristotle, *Meteorologica* 354a.

"a boundless continent." That there was a memory of a continent across the Atlantic is one of the most striking details suggesting that this account is not just fantasy.

Whether the Horseshoe Seamount Chain was really the site of Atlantis is a question for geologists and archaeologists to settle, but even in the case of this supposedly magnificent civilization, the absence of evidence is not as conclusive as one might think. The Greek historian Thucydides (c. 460–c. 400 B.C.), the first man in history to think about archaeology, observes about Sparta (also called Lacedaemon), "I suppose if Lacedaemon were to become desolate, and the temples and the foundations of the public buildings were left, that as time went on there would be a strong disposition with posterity to refuse to accept her fame as a true exponent of her power. And yet they occupy two-fifths of Peloponnese and lead the whole, not to speak of their numerous allies without. Still, as the city is neither built in a compact form nor adorned with magnificent temples and public edifices, but composed of villages after the old fashion of Hellas, there would be an impression of inadequacy."[6] Atlantis, too, could have been a great and comparatively advanced civilization that left few or no material remains.

---

[6]Thucydides, *The Peloponnesian War*, 1.10, trans. Richard Crawley: http://classics.mit.edu/Thucydides/pelopwar.1.first.html; accessed Jan. 13, 2011.

The legend of Atlantis was itself submerged in the West from the fifth to the fifteenth centuries A.D., when Plato's works were almost completely unknown. As his writings surfaced during the Renaissance, Atlantis attracted increasing speculation. Although the Bible—the supreme authority at that time—did not mention the vanished continent, it did speak of a great deluge, and on the face of it there was no reason this flood could not have engulfed Atlantis. Over the last five hundred years, the theories about the lost continent have been many and manifold, ranging from the plausible to the crazy. It is not possible to go into all, or even many, of them here. Readers might want to look at the book *Atlantis and the Cycles of Time* (published by Inner Traditions in 2010), by the British scholar of esotericism Joscelyn Godwin, which explores these views in depth.

One of the most important figures in comparatively recent times to talk about Atlantis was the Russian mystic H. P. Blavatsky, who discussed it in her compendious works *Isis Unveiled* and *The Secret Doctrine*. But Blavatsky's Atlantis is not the same as Plato's. Her intricate esoteric theory posited a number of "root races" that had preceded our own "Aryan" race. The Aryan race, in her view, was not limited to the Germanic or even to the Indo-European peoples but to practically the whole of humanity that has lived for the past million years. This Aryan root race was preceded by four others, two of which, the Chhaya [*sic*] and the Hyperborean, scarcely even made themselves manifest on the physical plane. The third and the fourth were Lemuria (named after another sunken continent that some nineteenth-century paleontologists believed to have been situated in the Indian Ocean) and Atlantis. Blavatsky wrote, "Up to this point of evolution [i.e., Atlantis, the fourth root race] man belongs more to metaphysical than physical nature. It is only after the so-called Fall that the races began to develop rapidly into a human shape," although, she adds, they were "much larger in size than we are now."[7]

The denizens of Atlantis had a fatal flaw, Blavatsky claimed. They were "marked with a character of Sorcery. . . . The Atlanteans of the later period were renowned for their magic powers and wickedness, their ambition and defiance of the gods."[8] It was this fatal flaw that led to their destruction by the element of water.

So far Blavatsky's account appears to correspond with Plato's, at least apart from the sorcery. But the time frame she gives for the rise and fall of Atlantis extends much further back than his. Indeed "the first Great flood . . .

---

[7] H. P. Blavatsky, *The Secret Doctrine* (London: Theosophical Publishing Co., 1888), 2:227n.

[8] Blavatsky, 2:286, 762. Capitalization in the original.

submerged the last portions of Atlantis, 850,000 years ago."[9]
The inhabitants of Plato's Atlantis were merely the last rem-
nant of the race, the Atlanteans' "degenerate descendants."[10]

Blavatsky's account has influenced many subsequent
pictures of Atlantis, particularly with its assertion that
Atlantis perished because its inhabitants misused occult
powers. Another highly influential view was that of the
American "sleeping prophet," Edgar Cayce, who in his
trance readings drew a picture of Atlantis that in many
ways resembled Blavatsky's, although his chronology was
different and much more recent: he claimed that Atlantis
was destroyed in three cataclysms in 58,000, 20,000, and
10,000 B.C. Like Blavatsky, Cayce said that Atlantis sank
because its inhabitants abused their powers. In the first
place, although of a spiritually higher caliber than those of
the preceding root races, the Atlanteans mated with them,
producing monstrous hybrids. The good Atlanteans, "Children of the Law of One," wanted to help the hybrids and
elevate them to their rightful position as children of God,
but another faction, the "Sons of Belial," treated the hybrids
as objects for sensual gratification.

The first destruction of Atlantis, said Cayce, was due
to a misuse of advanced technology for eliminating large

---

[9]Blavatsky, 2:332. Emphasis Blavatsky's.
[10]Blavatsky, 2:429.

carnivorous mammals that were overrunning the earth; the second, to a misuse of a "firestone" that gathered cosmic energy; the third, to a similar misuse of a crystal that employed both solar and geothermal power. This last destruction was complete by 9500 B.C.—a date very close to Plato's.

In a 1926 reading, Cayce mentioned the site of what he said had been the highest peaks in Atlantis—a pair of islands called Bimini, forty-five miles off the coast of Florida. For Cayce, it was (in his convoluted phrasing) "the highest portion left above the waves of a once great continent, upon which the civilization as now exists in the world's history [could] find much of that as would be used as a means for attaining that civilization [Atlantis]."[11]

Cayce also predicted major "earth changes"—a term that would resurface frequently in New Age circles—for the twentieth century. As he put it in 1940, "Poseidia (Atlantis) to rise again." (Poseidia was the name of the Atlantean capital in Plato's myth.) "Expect it in '68 and '69. Not so far away!"[12]

Indeed Cayce predicted titanic upheavals of land and sea between 1932 and 1998. These would begin, he claimed, "when there is the first breaking up of some conditions in

[11]In Mary Ellen Carter, *Edgar Cayce on Prophecy* (New York: Paperback Library, 1968), 117. Bracketed materials are in the original.
[12]Carter, 52.

the South Sea [i.e., the South Pacific] . . . and . . . the sink-
ing or rising of that which is almost opposite, or in the
Mediterranean, and the Aetna (Etna) area." But the
changes would be felt all over the world. "The greater portion of Japan must go into the sea. . . . The upper portion of
Europe will be changed as in the twinkling of an eye." In
America, "all over the country many physical changes of a
minor or greater degree. . . . Portions of the now east coast
of New York, or New York City itself, will in the main disappear. . . . The waters of the Great Lakes will empty into
the Gulf of Mexico."[13]

By now anyone who took the Cayce material at face
value must be disillusioned. The earth changes forecast for
the last two-thirds of the twentieth century did not happen. Someone who wants to maintain some belief in
Cayce's prophecies might point out that many of the earth
changes he foresaw resemble the long-term effects of
global warming, suggesting that he may have been right
about the events if not about the timing.

To step back from this tangle of legend, a person today
might draw some tentative conclusions. The geological
theory of plate tectonics—which shows that the continents
drift around the crust of the earth over a period spanning
geological ages—makes the idea of rising and falling con-

---

[13]Carter, 59–62.

tinents somewhat more plausible than it was a hundred years ago (although on a much larger time scale than Plato allows). In terms of the future, as I have already mentioned, predictions about the effects of global warming do bear certain resemblances to the prophecies of earth changes. Whether these will come true remains to be seen. In the meantime the best response is probably to stay both open-minded and sharply critical.

To return to a question posed at the outset: what about the fear that our civilization will be overcome by a cataclysm like the one that destroyed Atlantis? The fear is a present one. As I was writing this passage, I received an e-mail inviting me to speak in California in the autumn of 2011. The message reads, "We hope the times next fall will be convenient for you. If not, we can plan further out trusting that California won't be submerged or incinerated in 2012." The remark was tongue in cheek, but it reveals the hold of the idea over people's minds.

Concerns about a repetition of the fall of Atlantis are fed by another long-standing Western nightmare: the fear that the fall of the Roman Empire will happen again. This anxiety surfaces in curious places. A 1960 feature from the satirical magazine *Mad* tells us that "America is getting soft," to the point where our legs will dwindle down to vestigial features, making us easy targets for "the lean, hungry barbarians from the East." The accompanying cartoon shows a blank-faced American being pushed over like a round-bottomed doll by a gaunt and bucktoothed Red Chinese soldier.[14]

To turn to high culture, Edward Gibbon, whose eighteenth-century account of the decline and fall of the Roman Empire still remains the definitive version today, felt obliged to interrupt his history to prove that the fall of Rome could not happen again, partly because Western civilization had been transplanted to the Americas. "Should the victorious Barbarians carry slavery and desolation as far as the Atlantic Ocean," Gibbon wrote, "ten thousand vessels would transport beyond their pursuit the remains of civilized society; and Europe would revive and flourish in the American world which is already filled with her colonies and institutions."[15] He would not have mentioned this fear, or felt the need to refute it, unless it was vivid in the minds of his readers.

Still another layer of this collective fear lies in the dread of apocalypse inspired by biblical books such as Daniel and Revelation. Anxieties about the demise of our civilization thus go back as far as Western civilization itself. Today, taking on a multicultural form, they have fastened

[14]Dave Berg, "America Is Getting Soft," Mad 54 (April 1960), 25: http://blondesense.blogspot.com/2010/04/america-is-getting-soft.html; accessed Jan. 19, 2011.
[15]Edward Gibbon, The Decline and Fall of the Roman Empire, ch. 38.

onto notions of an end of time taken from native cultures (such as the 2012 sensation) and, in a secular context, to ecodisasters of one sort or another. Indeed one senses that anxiety of this kind is often encouraged by certain interest groups on the grounds that people will otherwise sit around in complacency.

I personally do not agree with this tactic. We have lived long enough with apocalypse, and we do not need updates of it to motivate us. People do not make the best decisions in moods of anxiety and panic. If we are to solve the problems that confront us, it will be by facing them soberly and realistically, without feeling the need to terrify ourselves into action.

To conclude with a prophecy of my own for the New Age: in the New Age, we will have to live without prophecies.

# Eight

# MASONIC CIVILIZATION

MASONRY. TO SOME, THE WORD connotes an underground cabal that, through means unknown and scarcely imaginable to ordinary mortals, topples governments and manipulates currencies. To others, more adept at observation than imagination, it evokes images of solid citizens in cheap suits congregating at the lodge on the second story of a shabby downtown commercial building.

In either case, today's seekers may wonder why Masonry should interest them. While some grain of esoteric knowledge may be buried in Masonry's peculiar rituals, how powerful could it be? The Masons we know—a father or an uncle, perhaps—so far from being mystic masters, usually blend unobtrusively into the background of middle-class life.

Personally I am not a Mason. I know no more of this tradition than can be found in books. Yet from the small amount of reading I've done, I'm convinced that every spiritual seeker today owes an incalculable debt to Freemasonry. You could even say that ours is fundamentally a Masonic civilization. (Freemasonry and Masonry, by the way, are more or less interchangeable terms; "the Craft" is a common nickname for it.) Hence it behooves us to try to pierce through the veil of misunderstanding and understand Masonry as it actually is. While there are many Masonries, each of which has its own color and flavor, in this article I will focus on the version that is most prevalent in the English-speaking world.

To understand why Masonry is so important, it's helpful to look at its origins—at least as far as we can glimpse them. The oldest known Masonic texts, the "Old Charges," which date to around 1400, set out a legendary heritage beginning with the antediluvian patriarch Jabal, who discovered geometry ("the which Science is called Massonrie") and wrote down his findings on pillars of stone. After Noah's Flood destroyed all human civilization, the Egyptian sage Hermes Trismegistus rediscovered this knowledge and passed it on in a lineage that includes Nimrod, Abraham, Euclid, and the eighty thousand masons who were said to have worked on Solomon's Temple.[1]

---

[1] David Stevenson, *The Origins of Freemasonry* (Cambridge: Cambridge University Press, 1988), 19–22.

Like many branches of the Western inner traditions, Masonry thus claims to go back to ancient Egypt and Israel. But most scholars today—including many Masons— would say there is no evidence of any such link. Most opt for one of two theories of Masonic origins.

The more romantic version holds that Freemasonry is a continuation of the vanished medieval order known as the Knights Templar.[2] Founded in 1118 to protect pilgrims journeying to the Holy Land, the Templars soon became a major force in the Crusades, helping to reconquer Palestine from the Saracens and keep it in Christian hands. The Templars soon outstripped their original purpose and grew into the most powerful military and economic force in Christendom. But by the end of the thirteenth century, their wealth and prestige had made them suspect to many of the sacred and secular powers. When the Holy Land fell back into Muslim hands in 1291, the Templars seemed to have lost their reason for existence.

Not long thereafter, King Philip the Fair of France determined to lay his hands on the Templars' wealth. With the connivance of Pope Clement V, Philip contrived to have the order suppressed and its properties confiscated.

---

[2]See John J. Robinson, *Born in Blood: The Lost Secrets of Freemasonry* (New York: M. Evans, 1989) and Michael Baigent and Richard Leigh, *The Temple and the Lodge* (London: Jonathan Cape, 1989). A far more speculative work is Christopher Knight and Robert Lomas, *The Hiram Key: Pharaohs, Freemasonry, and the Discovery of the Secret Scrolls of Jesus* (Rockport, Mass.: Element, 1996).

On Friday, October 13, 1307 (a date which some believe gave rise to the popular fear of Friday the thirteenth), mass arrests were carried out on the French Templars. In 1312, the order was dissolved; and in 1314, Jacques de Molay, the last Templar Grand Master, was burned at the stake in Paris.

The charges against the Templars were extremely peculiar. They were accused of both sodomy and heresy, and it was said that they worshiped an idol named Baphomet and required initiates to spit on the crucifix. These charges were almost certainly trumped up; in true medieval fashion, they were extracted by torture. Given that the Templars' courage in defending Christendom during the Crusades was never in dispute, the charges of disloyalty to the faith are hard to believe.

Certain researchers contend that not all the Templars were arrested. Some of them, forewarned, managed to make their way to Scotland, whose king was at the time under excommunication by Rome (and hence was not bound by the papal suppression) and which was fighting to keep its independence from England (and hence needed good soldiers). Taking refuge there, the Templars hid their identity and perpetuated their esoteric teaching under the guise of a stonemasons' guild.

If this theory is true, the Templar tradition went resolutely underground for some three hundred years before

resurfacing in the guise of Masonry. There is some resonance to the Templar legacy, and Masons themselves have
invoked it. The highest level of York Rite Masonry (a series
of Masonic higher degrees) is named "Order of the Knights
Templar," and the young persons' Masonic organization is
known as De Molay. But there are numerous problems
with this theory—the biggest one being the circumstanti-
ality of the evidence. Proponents of "alternative history"
have made much of Templar–Mason connections, without
firm substantiation. Advocates of this theory have been
taken to task for their highly speculative conclusions based
on little evidence, often oblivious to records that state the
opposite.[3]

A less romantic, but far more plausible, view is that
Masonry evolved from the old stonemasons' guilds of
the Middle Ages, which often included moral and religious teachings along with practical instruction. As the medieval order began to break down, these guilds gradually
took in members who did not belong to the masons' trade.
These newcomers often included gentlemen who were
intrigued by the philosophical doctrines they thought
might be hidden in the masons' craft. Eventually this
"speculative Masonry" displaced the earlier "operative

---

[3]See Jay Kinney, *The Masonic Myth: Unlocking the Truth About the Symbols, the
Secret Rites, and the History of Freemasonry* (San Francisco: Harper One, 2009),
ch. 2, for a balanced discussion of these issues.

Masonry" of the lodges, and modern Freemasonry was born.

At any rate the first surviving evidence regarding Masonic lodges comes from Scotland around the turn of the seventeenth century.[4] At this time, the Scottish lodges were still primarily "operative," although lodge members' lists indicate that they began to include a trickle of worthies and gentlemen.

Within a few decades, speculative Masonry began to emerge in England, where a number of esotericists had gathered in flight from the Thirty Years' War raging in Germany. These men were associated with the "Rosicrucian enlightenment," alluding to the mysterious Brothers of the Rosy Cross, an occult fraternity tracing its origin to an elusive and possibly fictitious adept known as Christian Rosenkreutz ("Rose Cross"). The existence of this order was proclaimed in some anonymous pamphlets published around 1614 and known as the Rosicrucian manifestoes. But the Rosicrucian brothers never made a public appearance, despite many efforts to track them down. Nevertheless, they were connected in the popular mind with Kabbalistic and Hermetic teachings that were already very much in vogue in the early modern era, and to which many European intellectuals of the time adhered.

---

[4] See Stevenson for an account of Masonry's Scottish origins.

These two threads, the operative tradition preserved in Scotland and the Rosicrucian ideas that had been brought from the Continent, probably produced modern Freemasonry as we know it. By the early seventeenth century, Masonry begins to enter the public scene, and we encounter records of lodge meetings in several Scottish towns. By 1638, a Scottish poet named Henry Adamson could write:

> For what we do presage is not in grosse,
> For we be brethren of the Rosie Crosse;
> We have the Mason word, and second sight;
> Things for to come we can foretell aright.[5]

It might be overinterpreting to say that Adamson was specifically connecting the Masons with the Rosicrucians; he may simply have been playing with associated ideas, just as a satirist today might lump the 2012 furor together with Atlantis and crystal skulls without believing they necessarily have anything to do with one another. But this reference proves that both the Masons and the Rosicrucians were well known among the literate public—at least in Scotland—by Adamson's time.

There is other evidence for a Masonic-Rosicrucian link. One of the most influential of the seventeenth-century

---

[5]Frances Yates, *The Rosicrucian Enlightenment* (London: Ark, 1972), 211.

speculative Masons was an Englishman named Elias Ashmole, who was initiated in 1646. Ashmole, a noted anti-
quarian (his collection forms the nucleus of Oxford's
Ashmolean Museum), was also one of the founders of the
Royal Society, the first modern organization for scientific
investigation. Before its establishment in 1660, the group's
members, meeting informally, called themselves "the Invisible College"—a term taken from the Rosicrucian manifestoes. Nearly all of the Royal Society's first members were
Masons.[6]

After this point, Masonic history becomes more a matter of record and less of conjecture. After the Grand Lodge
of London (today known as the United Grand Lodge of
England) was formed in 1717, Masonic history enters into
the spotlight. Its influence on the American and French
revolutions of the eighteenth century is indisputable, as
was its role in the unification of Italy in the nineteenth: the
leading figure in the reunification was Giuseppe Garibaldi,
who was also Grand Master of the Italian lodge. Since
then, Freemasonry has been one of the chief sponsors of
republican government against monarchism and of rational, scientific investigation as opposed to ecclesiastical
dogma. But is this all it comes to? I think not. It's worth
trying to understand why.

---

[6]Yates, 171–92, 210–11.

Western civilization, for all its greatness, has never entirely succeeded in reconciling the sacred with the secular. Christianity, persecuted by both the Jewish and the Roman authorities, hardly had a healthy relationship with the worldly powers in its formative years. When it almost accidentally became the state religion of the Roman Empire in the fourth century A.D., the Christian Church was ill-prepared for the role. In later centuries Eastern Orthodoxy would turn into an arm of the Byzantine and tsarist states, while Catholicism, stepping into the vacuum created by the collapse of the Western Empire, began to intrude into the realm of secular power.

By the thirteenth century, popes like Innocent III were not only temporal lords (ruling most of central Italy) but were claiming universal sovereignty; they regarded secular monarchs like the Holy Roman Emperor as mere vassals. (The emperors themselves, of course, never quite saw things this way, leading to some of the greatest political struggles of the Middle Ages.)

It was in this atmosphere that the Templars were dissolved. The popes and bishops were alternately manipulating, and manipulated by, the kings and emperors of Europe, and corruption flourished on a scale that makes our present-day scandals look puny. Whatever truth there may have been to the idea of Templar heresies, the chief motive for their dissolution was probably the authorities' greed for their wealth.

Friday the thirteenth of October, 1307, was the day the sacred and secular powers chose to descend upon the Templars, and for Western civilization it was a very unlucky day indeed. For the Templar dissolution seemed to be final proof that, despite the considerable spiritual power the Catholic Church possessed and continues to possess, it could not be trusted in matters secular.

Since that time, if you grant some kind of Templar-Masonic link, the heirs to the Templar lineage in both Europe and America have fought to separate secular from sacred authority. This struggle was not won in a day or even a century; religious tolerance was a distant dream for many centuries after the Templars were jailed.

Masonry and Roman Catholicism were not always mutually exclusive, and some early Masonic texts even enjoin members to be loyal to the Church. Nor does Masonry dispute the spiritual teachings of the Catholic Church; its requirement of a belief in a Supreme Being and a life after death are perfectly consistent with Catholicism. But by its insistence on respect for all religions, Freemasonry does challenge Catholic (and all other) claims to an exclusive monopoly on spiritual truth; only in the sense that it undercuts the doctrine *extra ecclesiam nulla salus* ("No salvation outside the church") can it be called anti-Catholic. (For similar reasons it frightens many Protestant fundamentalists.) But since 1738, when Pope Clement XII issued the bull *In eminenti* condemning Free-masonry, Catholics have been forbidden to become Masons.

Given that modern science and modern democracy—both of which have always enjoyed only equivocal support from the Catholic Church—have Masonic origins, it's not entirely far-fetched to contend that ours is a Masonic civilization. This is not to say that it is free from abuses of its own. Like the medieval Christian civilization that preceded it, the modern Masonic civilization presents its own problems: representative government is prone to corruption, while scientific materialism has spawned its own weird form of bigotry. These excesses, if they go unchecked, may call for another response from the "conscious circle of humanity" much like the one that gave rise to Masonry. In the long run, Masonic civilization is probably, like its predecessors, only one stage in an enormous program of constructing a grand Temple of human experience, whose nature and goal we today can barely guess at.

Is there a Masonic conspiracy juggling world events behind the scenes? I, of course, have no way of knowing, but to all appearances, Masonry is less influential than it was a century ago. I suspect that there are circles in which Masonic affiliation may help as a means to advancement—but that's a far cry from saying it's a dark web of international evil. Connections in the old boys' network and the power elite are probably far more influential in personal advancement than Masonic rings or secret handshakes—as they probably are in global political and business decisions.

But let's turn away from these grand perspectives and ask what Masonry offers in a spiritual sense. There are many interpretations of Masonic rites, symbols, and degrees; some are more plausible and authoritative than others, but none is taken as an absolute within Masonry itself. This suggests not only that Masonry has tried to avoid slavery to creeds and formulations, but that the ultimate meaning of its rituals lies in the rites themselves. That is to say, their import is not some kind of implicit verbal message, but the effect they have on the being of the candidate. Carried out properly, the rites should leave their own distinct mark on the individual on both conscious and unconscious levels.

For me, the most fascinating of the Masonic mysteries has to do with the Master Mason ritual, which recounts the story of the death of Hiram Abiff. In this legend, Hiram works as the chief architect of Solomon's Temple.[7] Three "ruffians" conspire to extract the secret of the Master Mason from him. One day, as Hiram tries to leave the site of the unfinished Temple through the south entrance, he is stopped by the first ruffian. Armed with a rule, the ruffian demands the secret. Hiram refuses, and the ruffian strikes him with the rule on his right temple. He sinks down onto his left knee.

Hiram then rushes to the west gate, where he is accosted by the second ruffian, who holds a level. Confronted with the same request, Hiram again refuses and is struck on the left temple with this tool. He falls onto his right knee. Now Hiram, faint and bleeding, staggers to the east entrance, where the third ruffian is posted. Being refused as well, he hits Hiram on the forehead with a heavy stone maul, which finally kills him.

The ruffians bury Hiram in "the rubbish of the Temple," later exhuming him to give him a more permanent burial under an acacia tree to the west of the site. King Solomon and another Hiram, king of Tyre, dispatch a search for the lost master. A group of workmen find him, and Solomon gives Hiram Abiff his third and final burial near the Holy of Holies of the uncompleted Temple.

---

[7] A worker named Hiram is mentioned in the biblical account of the Temple's construction, 1 Kings 7:13–45; 2 Chron. 2:13–4:18. But he is a worker in brass, not an architect, and there is no reference to his murder.

Solomon raises a monument to him in the form of a virgin weeping over a broken column and holding a sprig of acacia; behind her is the figure of Time with a scythe; he holds a snake to her head. With Hiram dead, the Temple will remain unfinished until one who knows the "Master's Word" can complete it.[8]

What could this strange tale possibly mean? I will try to give one interpretation here. It is not meant to be definitive; as I've said, such a thing is probably impossible. What I'm about to say owes a great deal to an account in Harold W. Percival's fascinating and compendious 1946 book *Thinking and Destiny*, but it is not identical to Percival's account.[9]

Hiram is consciousness. The Temple that he is building is the true Self, the complete and integrated human being. The three ruffians are the three ordinary functions that operate in man, frequently characterized as thinking, feeling, and doing. Now these functions, the three ruffians, work together at least well enough to plot against Hiram. But because they are unintegrated and unconscious themselves, they cannot attain their goal. In fact they only end

---

[8]Knight and Lomas, 9–17. In some versions, the first two blows fall on Hiram's shoulder and the nape of his neck. See Edmond Gloton, *Instruction maçonnique aux Maîtres-Maçons* (Paris: V. Gloton, 1950), 56–57.

[9]Harold W. Percival, *Thinking and Destiny* (Dallas, Tex.: Word Foundation, 1946), 680–86. See also W. Kirk MacNulty, *Freemasonry: A Journey through Ritual and Symbol* (London: Thames & Hudson, 1991), 28–30.

up "killing" the consciousness, that is, making it descend into the oblivion of ordinary life.

There are also higher functions in man, symbolized by Solomon and Hiram of Tyre. They do not have the secret of consciousness either. But they can at least set up a memorial—that is, a reminder that something has been lost. Until it is found, man is subject to the forces of time and delusion (symbolized by the serpent).

Interestingly, the three ruffians are named Jubelo, Jubela, and Jubelum. The first part of the names is obviously akin to Jabal, discoverer of "the Science called Massonrie," while the suffixes resemble Latin masculine, feminine, and neuter endings. But as Percival notes, there is another dimension to these endings. If you put them together, you have "Aoum," or the sacred syllable "Om," which Percival equates with the true Mason's word. That is to say, the three ruffians, the inferior functions of man, possess part of the secret of consciousness. But they do not have the secret of integrating them and bringing them to the higher level symbolized by the Temple.

If Masonry is a true initiatic tradition, it contains within its rites and teachings and symbols the means to restore this lost word and bring the Temple to perfection. (I am told that this is part of the Royal Arch ritual, one of the many higher degrees of Masonry.)

I personally do not have the experience to say whether

Masonry, now or ever, has possessed the secret of restoring the "lost word" of consciousness. But the Masonic tradition has been a prime inspiration for many of the esoteric teachings of recent centuries. The Theosophist H. P. Blavatsky was greatly indebted to it; she even claimed to have been initiated as a Mason herself in an irregular order on the Continent. ("Regular" Masonry—consisting of lodges that are recognized by the United Grand Lodge of England—does not admit women.) The founders of the Victorian magical society known as the Hermetic Order of the Golden Dawn were all high-degree Masons. Some forms of Wicca, the updated descendant of the ancient pagan religion of the British Isles, have three degrees of initiation, very likely inspired by the first three degrees of Freemasonry.

This leads us back, perhaps, to the notion of conspiracy; paranoids may shriek that here is more evidence of some grand plot to lure humankind toward the lairs of Satan. For my part I can see no such thing; indeed if there is a worldwide conspiracy to increase consciousness and promote tolerance, scientific inquiry, and representative government, I can only regret that it has not proved stronger.

## Nine

# A COURSE IN MIRACLES
## REVISITED

IN SPIRITUAL TEACHINGS, as in any human endeavor, mass success is not a guide to true worth. On the other hand, to dismiss anything that appeals to more than the tiniest of audiences is equally unfounded. With no current teaching, perhaps, does this observation hold more true than with *A Course in Miracles*. Over the last thirty-five years, this strange work has sold more than one-and-a-half million copies, chiefly by word of mouth. It has begotten an entire subculture of organizations, newsletters, and conferences, even sects, schisms, and controversies (chiefly over copyright issues). It has been called the only sacred text whose native language is English. It has also been dismissed as a mere rehash of the New Age positive-thinking philosophy.

From any point of view, the story of the *Course* is a strange one. In 1965, Helen Schucman, a professor of medical psychology at Columbia University's College of Physicians and Surgeons, began to hear an inner voice urging her to take dictation it was about to give for "a course in miracles." Fearing for her sanity, she consulted a colleague, who suggested that since she was otherwise perfectly functional, perhaps she should simply take down the dictation as instructed.

What Schucman wrote down over the next several years turned into a massive work, comprising three volumes: a Text setting out the theory of the *Course*; a Workbook containing 365 daily lessons that would enable the student to put the ideas into practice; and a brief Manual for Teachers that answered some common questions and defined some terms. Privately circulated during the early 1970s, the *Course* made its way into print in 1975.

All of this would be of minor interest except that voice inside Schucman's head claimed to be that of Jesus Christ, and the teaching a radical revisioning of Christianity. The voice also said that this was Christ's original teaching, which the Apostles had in certain respects gotten wrong. Schucman herself never claimed the work as her own, and indeed displayed a certain ambivalence about it for the rest of her life; she died in 1981.

Certainly there is no shortage of material dictated by voices inside people's heads, but whatever else the *Course* may or may not be, it is *not* a collection of paranoid ravings. Quite the opposite: it is not only intelligent but profound. It is also endowed with a rare eloquence (although it is printed as prose, much of the work scans perfectly as blank verse).

The *Course's* doctrine is difficult to summarize, but the essential points can be boiled down as follows. Like many of the great spiritual traditions, the *Course* teaches that the world we see has no intrinsic reality. It is the result of "a tiny, mad idea, at which the Son of God remembered not to laugh" (T, 544). This "tiny, mad idea" was the deluded thought that anything could exist apart from God. By entertaining this thought of separation, the Son of God—who is collectively the human race—shattered into billions of tiny fragments. These are the individual selves that we imagine ourselves to be. This illusory separation gave rise to the world we see with the body's eyes—ultimately meaningless, engendered by and engendering nothing but fear.

In his mercy, God did not leave the Sonship adrift in its own terrors. The instant that this "tiny, mad idea" appeared, God produced a response, which the *Course* identifies with the Holy Spirit, whose purpose is to bridge the apparent gap between God and man. The plan for restoring the shattered Sonship is called the Atonement. When the Atonement is complete—that is, when all the Sons of God are fully aware of their unity with God and with one another—the world will end, as will the artificial constructs of time and space. The world has value or meaning only as a kind of framework in which the Son of God (that is to say, all of us) can recall his essential unity with God and return to the "real world" that God *did* create—a world in which there is no separation, suffering, or loss. There is no damnation and no punishment: God condemns no one. "The world will end in laughter, because it is a place of tears" (M, 36).

Since the *Course* claims to be the work of Jesus Christ, in it Jesus usually speaks in the first person. He does not claim any special status as a Son of God, since we are all equally part of the Sonship. He is simply the first human being to have fully accepted his role in the Atonement. The Manual for Teachers asks rhetorically about Jesus: "Is he the Son of God? O yes, along with you" (M, 83).

Taken on its own terms, the *Course*'s worldview is remarkably logical and self-consistent. Moreover, it echoes a number of ancient esoteric teachings. With its depiction of a collective Sonship, which includes all human beings past and present, the *Course* resembles the Kabbalah, with its concept of Adam Kadmon, the primordial man; Emanuel Swedenborg's doctrine of the *maximus homo* or "Universal Human"; and even the Catholic dogma of the Mystical Body of Christ.

The *Course*'s chief method of "healing the dream" of

separation is forgiveness. Since there is no true separation between individuals, one can never hold a grievance against someone else without holding it against oneself at some level. The *Course* also stresses that God did not create evil; it is the result of the deluded Sonship imagining that it is, or could be, separate from God. If evil has no real existence in itself, the only proper response to it in any and every instance is to overlook it—through forgiveness.

"God is in everything I see," says an early lesson in the Workbook. The lesson goes on to say, "Try, then, today to begin to learn how to look on all things with love, appreciation, and open-mindedness. You do not see them now. . . . Nothing is as it appears to you. Its holy purpose stands beyond your little range. When vision has shown you the holiness that lights up the world, you will understand today's idea perfectly" (W, 45). By practices of this kind, the *Course* intends to open the student's mind to an experience of the "real world" that lies behind our projections of fear.

The tremendous interest and commitment the *Course* has aroused is almost entirely the result of word of mouth. The established churches have shown virtually no interest in it, and the more conservative theologians predictably dismiss it as a collection of heresies, usually of the Gnostic variety. While some congregations have grown up around the *Course*, the majority of its students meet in informal groups often numbering a dozen or even less, often held in people's homes. Many of these regard the *Course* as their primary spiritual path.

From my personal point of view (I have worked with this material since 1981), I have been invariably impressed with both the profundity and the practicality of the *Course*. Its chief goal is to put the student in touch with a level of inner guidance that it equates with the voice of the Holy Spirit. While I have known people who have taken this idea to extremes, my experience suggests that the *Course*, if practiced sincerely and carefully, can provide a student with remarkably constant access to a deep level of inner wisdom.

I find it both curious and entirely understandable that the *Course* has left such a faint mark on mainstream religion. On the one hand, it offers one of the most powerful and creative perspectives on issues ranging from the nature of evil to the nature of Christ that we have seen in recent times. On the other hand, its peculiar origins ensure that the professional theologians will be reluctant to be seen with it, much less discuss it seriously. It is bound to seem "unto the Greeks foolishness." Nor has it always been well served by its popularizers, who have focused on its feel-good aspects while glossing over the rigorous inner sincerity and discipline required to engage fully with the *Course*.

Whether the *Course* is or is not accepted by the authorities and the public at large is, in the end, of no great importance. Like many powerful teachings over the course of the centuries, the *Course* has gone directly to open minds that welcome it. Consequently, thirty years after entering the collective discourse, *A Course in Miracles* remains influential but elusive, dwelling outside the convenient pigeonholes of religious categorization and challenging Christianity at large to come up with something better than its current standard fare. Perhaps that is what its author—whoever that may have been—originally intended.

### SOURCES

References to *A Course in Miracles* are to the first edition (Tiburon, Calif.: Foundation for Inner Peace, 1975). T = Text; W = Workbook; M = Manual for Teachers.

# Ten

# HIDDEN MASTERS

HIDDEN MASTERS FORM PART OF A long tradition in esoteric lore. Many have claimed that they have seen and met adepts who, having reached much higher levels of realization than ordinary people, are able to appear and disappear at will.

The tradition is an ancient one. The Jewish Kabbalists hold that the prophet Elijah, who ascended to heaven in a fiery chariot, still appears to those who have reached a certain level of attainment. The Muslim equivalent is Khidr, the mysterious "Green Man" alluded to in the Qur'an, who also makes his presence felt to those who are ripe for the experience.

In the West, the idea of hidden masters first surfaced in Germany around 1615, when the publication of two pamphlets called the *Fama fraternitatis* ("The Rumor of the Brotherhood") and the *Confessio fraternitatis* ("The Confession of the Brotherhood") sent the educated world into a frenzy. The pamphlets spoke of a mysterious Rosicrucian brotherhood, a society of adepts founded by one Christian Rosenkreutz, who had gained occult knowledge in his journeys to the East. The pamphlets promised that the brotherhood would be open to those who proclaimed their interest. A flurry of pamphlets followed from authors professing their devotion to the society's ideals, but to our knowledge no one made contact with the brothers. As a result, they were nicknamed the "Invisibles." In later centuries, various organizations laid claim to the Rosicrucian heritage. Many are still in existence, but it is far from clear that any of them have a genuine, organic connection to the Rosicrucians of the seventeenth century.

Whoever and whatever the Rosicrucian masters were, they did not materialize in front of their pupils. In the modern world, the concept of hidden masters owes its popularity to Helena Petrovna Blavatsky. Blavatsky claimed that she first made contact with one of the masters, a "tall Hindu," during a visit to England in 1851. In 1875, allegedly under the guidance of some of these masters, she and her associate Henry Steel Olcott founded the Theosophical Society in New York.

Skeptics usually argue that Blavatsky's masters were a fraud concocted by her, but this contention is hard to support in anything like a pure form. The masters did not appear only to Blavatsky. C. W. Leadbeater, an Anglican clergyman who later became one of the leaders of the Theosophical Society, describes his first encounter with a master:

> The door of the room was in full sight, and it certainly did not open; but quite suddenly, without any preparation, there was a man standing almost between me and Madame Blavatsky, within touch of both of us. It gave me a great start, and I jumped up in some confusion. Madame Blavatsky was much amused and said: "If you do not know enough not to be startled at such a trifle as that, you will not get far in this occult work."

Nor did the masters appear only in Blavatsky's presence. Olcott reported that one night, having retired to his room, he saw "towering above me in his great stature an Oriental clad in white garments," who advised Olcott that "a great work was to be done for humanity" and that Olcott could share in it if he wished. Despite his awe, Olcott wondered silently if Blavatsky had not cast some kind of "hypnotic glamour" over him. As if in response, the majestic personage removed his head cloth and left it behind as a souvenir before vanishing.

Contact with the masters continued, extending far

beyond Theosophical circles. In 1919, an Englishwoman named Alice Bailey was telepathically contacted by a master named D.K. (or "Djwhal Kul"), who was said to be among the circle of adepts that worked with Blavatsky and Olcott. For the next thirty years, Bailey would serve as D.K.'s amanuensis, transcribing works he was dictating from the remoteness of his monastery in the Himalayas. An American businessman named Guy Ballard said he met the master known as the Comte de St.-Germain while hiking on Mount Shasta in northern California in 1930. On the basis of St.-Germain's revelations, Ballard started the "I AM" movement. A direct descendant is the Church Universal and Triumphant of Elizabeth Clare Prophet, who says she has received numerous transmissions from similar masters. Today many New Agers believe they have had contact with these masters. Some are clearly deluded; others may not be.

Who, then, are the masters? What explains their nature or their powers—if they actually exist? Opinions vary. The Theosophists have generally claimed that their masters exist in a physical body, although they are much more capable of putting on and taking off these vehicles than are ordinary mortals. Leadbeater writes, "In the majority of cases, one who gains that level no longer needs a physical body. He no longer retains an astral, a mental or even a causal body, but lives permanently at his higher level.

Whenever for any purpose he needs to deal with a lower plane, he must take a temporary vehicle belonging to that plane." The Web site of Prophet's Summit Lighthouse says something similar about the masters: "Though they once had physical bodies like we wear, they now dwell in the heaven world, or etheric octave, and have bodies of light."

The theories behind this phenomenon grow quite elaborate, and to discuss them in detail one would almost have to explain the whole of Theosophy, say, or of *A Course in Miracles*. But the basic point is simple. Materiality, this physical world that seems so hard and solid to us, is far more malleable than we customarily believe. It is simply the topmost of innumerable layers of existence that are composed of increasingly subtle and refined levels of thought. One who has conscious access to these levels has an apparently miraculous power over the denser ones, including, it is said, the ability to materialize and dematerialize at will.

Personally, I have never experienced such a phenomenon; if I did, I'm sure I would find it extremely disorienting. But I have enough experience of the fluid and ambiguous nature of reality that I am far from willing to dismiss the idea of hidden masters as entirely a hoax or delusion.

*Eleven*

# CULTIVATING THE FIELD
# OF IMAGES

PARADISE IS A GARDEN, we are told, and anyone who has contemplated the serenity of a well-managed landscape can appreciate the appeal of this idea. The human hand, with its shovel and shears, imposes a firm but gentle control on the rugged growths of nature, molding the terrain as a sculptor works with stone or metal; each plant and shrub has its place in a masterfully planned order. Such harmony must have even more allure for those who live surrounded by the brown aridity of the desert, as the authors of the Bible did, and it is easy to understand why Genesis portrays God as strolling in Eden in the cool of the day.

And yet even the tamest garden is a jungle rife with Darwinian struggle; each flower and herb has to fight off weeds and pests and parasites. Unlike the warfare of the animal kingdom, which makes itself heard in bleats and roars and snarls, this struggle is a silent one, but it is no less savage. Human intelligence may tip the balance in favor of its own predilections, but if this control slips for even a short while, the forces of overgrowth assert themselves again.

Is this really what sacred texts like Genesis envision? Conventional theology holds—or used to hold—that Eden was a "terrestrial paradise," as Dante called it. Perhaps—but there is another teaching that is worth hearing in this context. Some traditions hold that the primordial garden of delight lies not on earth but in another dimension altogether.

This idea is echoed in the myths of many peoples. The Greeks' Garden of the Hesperides, although said to be located to the west of the Pillars of Hercules, is not really an earthly realm but a heavenly one; here "the good enjoy a life free from sorrow, having the sun both day and night," as Pindar puts it. The Shambhala of the Tibetans, a realm on the threshold between this reality and another, and hopelessly impenetrable to all but the pure-hearted, is a similar instance. So is Belovodye, the "Land of White Waters" rumored to lie hidden somewhere in the Altai Mountains of Siberia; so are the Lyonesse and Avalon of the Arthurian cycle. All these kingdoms are both of this world and not of this world. Like the reality we know, they are realms of forms and colors and shapes; but there is some radical difference as well, something that sets them apart from the earthly dimension and makes it impossible to situate them on a map.

These traditions come into focus if we see them, not as memories of lost civilizations or travelers' tall tales passed down at third and fourth hand, but as representations of what is called the imaginal realm—the world of thoughts and dreams and images, the dimension of the "astral light," what the Kabbalists know as Yetzirah or the world of formation.

Such an interpretation helps us to understand the tales of these elusive paradises. The physical world will always have its hardships and disappointments. Lack and abundance alternate relentlessly, and apprehension about the future always steals some measure of joy from the present. In the imaginal world it is not so. Here, one might say, is the Wish-Fulfilling Gem of which the Buddhists speak, for all one has to do is to think of something in order to possess it. In this dimension, desire and satisfaction are inextricably bound, and any suffering that can be thought of is immediately relieved by imagining its cure.

This, then, may be the garden of delight of which the Bible speaks ("Eden" meaning "delight"). And, as we all know, if such a place exists, we seem hopelessly estranged from it. On earth there is always some gap, sometimes short, sometimes intolerably long, between a need and its fulfillment. Even when our desires are granted, it is usually only partially and as it were grudgingly. How did we find ourselves in this situation?

Part of the answer may be suggested by the verse in Genesis that says "the Lord God took the man, and put him into the garden of Eden to dress it and to keep it" (Gen. 2:15). The primal task of humanity, then, is to serve as a caretaker for this realm. To understand what this "gardening" may involve, we might consider an idea that appears more prominently in Islam than in Judaism or Christianity. Certain Muslim esotericists, notably Ibn 'Arabi, distinguish the "imaginal" realm from the "imaginary" as we usually experience it.

What is the difference? Possibly the dream state, which is the most familiar form in which humans interact with this level, can offer some insight. Practically all the dreams we have are reflections of the twistings and turnings of our own minds. The complex and allusive language of dream imagery vividly depicts our desires, fears, and conflicts. As Nietzsche observed, "Every man is a great artist in his dreams."

Such is the ordinary life of our consciousness in sleep. Its artistic power, though awesome, is also strangely evanescent, and we find ourselves hard put even to remember these astonishing creations when we wake in the morning. This could be associated with *imagination* per se.

Occasionally, though, we manage to slip through to a higher level of the dream experience. Here we have a sense, not that we are indulging in our own spontaneous acts of mental creation, but that we have entered into another dimension that is no less objectively real than that of the physical, and indeed does not differ from it except in being incomparably more beautiful and satisfying. Such experiences may take the form of lucid dreams or even of a sense of out-of-body travel. While we may not know what to make of these experiences later, they do leave the haunting and ineradicable impression that there are more facets to reality than we normally believe. This, one could say, is the level of the *imaginal*.

While the realm of the imaginal is real—a fact that seems both experientially true and has been confirmed by the teachings of mystics and esotericists—we are usually cut off from it. Our glimpses of it are rare, and we would probably not believe in it at all if the experiences themselves did not have such power and authority. And what seems to separate us from this imaginal level is the imaginary. That is to say, our own uncontrolled fantasies and daydreams and desires are what stand in the way of our access to higher consciousness.

In the light of this idea, we might be able to go back to the suggestion that man was originally meant to serve as a gardener. The mind, as we all know, has a spontaneous, self-creative power. There is something dynamic and relentless in its capacity to produce images and emotions. In this it resembles the vegetable kingdom, which seems to grow and multiply at a prodigious rate unless it is managed by intelligent cultivation. And this, it seems to me, is what the metaphor of the garden and the gardener is ultimately about. The human race seems to have been created as a steward for this intermediate realm. "Keeping the garden" would have to do with keeping a careful watch over the dimension of imagination—tending and fostering those that are suitable, cutting out those that are unwholesome.

But of course this is precisely what we do *not* do. We constantly fall prey to our own imaginings; the mind is wild, careless, and wanton. This may give at least one meaning of the story of the Fall. The primal man and woman, created to tend the garden of the mind, became fascinated by its products. They wished to "know good and evil," and of course the only way one can truly know something is to experience it directly. So the human race has been collectively exiled to the dimension we know, where we live not among images that can be easily molded by thought and will, but among the hard-edged objects of physicality. And imagination itself has been unleashed. It creates fantasies and dreams willy-nilly, sometimes lovely, often ugly or terrifying, and we have lost recollection of ourselves to the point where we are inundated and over-powered by them.

If this interpretation is correct, it casts some light on one central focus of many spiritual traditions—the need to control the mind. Our spontaneous and seemingly un-stoppable capacity to generate ideas and thoughts must be arrested or at least brought under rein. This is the first tenet of Patanjali's *Yoga Sutras*: *Yoga citta vritti nirodha*: "Yoga is the cessation of the oscillations of the mind." *A Course in Miracles* puts it more bluntly: "You are much too tolerant of mind wandering, and are passively condoning your mind's miscreations." Only when the garden of the imagination is properly tended can we glimpse the higher realm of the imaginal.

Will this kind of mental discipline restore the peace and equilibrium we so desperately seek? For all the books and tapes and lectures on meditation, it still remains true that this solution, however promising, is almost never really tried. Probably it cannot be truly achieved in the course of modern life, which not only offers distractions but seems to be deliberately engineered to construct them.

All the same there is, I suspect, much advantage to be gained from the simple observation that these fantasies and fears which preoccupy us so unwearyingly are little more than phantasms. Every once in a while life hits us with a shock to remind us of this truth. We realize we have been girding ourselves for a struggle that has never materialized, or that we have lost much sleep dreading a confrontation that never took place. At such junctures we have the chance to glimpse how much of our inner lives has little to do with anything real on any level.

There is a problem with this line of thinking. One can easily start to demonize the imagination, turning it into the great villain of life. There is always something dangerous—and false—in blaming all one's woes on a single part of one's being (as was done with the body for many centuries). The imagination, even in its most uncontrolled forms, is also the generator of great works of vision in art, science, and every other arena of human achievement. To deny this or to try to completely stifle the mind's creative dynamism is to risk turning into something like Mr. Gradgrind in Dickens's *Hard Times*—"a man of facts and calculations. A man who proceeds upon the principle that two and two are four, and nothing over, and who is not to be talked into allowing for anything over."

Even so it seems to be our fate to fall prey over and over again to the traps of our fantasies. The sacred traditions speak of a collective Fall that caused this situation; they also allude to some future state where these mistakes will be remedied and humanity will be free from its long oppression. This coming eventuality is symbolized by the countless legends of Last Judgments, apocalypses, and messianic ages that abound in religious lore. It is also symbolized, in a somewhat less grandiose way, by tales of death and resurrection. The divine hero—who is, of course, each of us—suffers passions and tribulations and even death; but in the end it is of no account; he appears again in a newer, higher, and possibly unfamiliar form. As John's Gospel says, Mary Magdalene at first fails to recognize the risen Christ, "supposing him to be the gardener."

*Twelve*

# THE SCIENCE OF
# THOUGHT

I F THERE IS A CENTRAL religious doctrine for the New
Age, surely it is this—the belief that positive thoughts
can bend reality to their own shape.

It is an alluring concept. If it's true, we don't need to act
or work or perform in the world. All we need to do is
change our thinking. But is there anything to this idea?

To understand something about the doctrine of thought
power, it's helpful to look at its history. The father of the
religion of positive thinking was an obscure New En-
glander named Phineas Parkhurst Quimby (1802–1866).
Quimby, like many men of his time, was a jack of all
trades. He started as a clockmaker, but eventually became
fascinated with alternative methods of healing and learned
the art of mesmerism or animal magnetism, a forerunner
of hypnosis. Quimby found that if he put an assistant into
a trance, the assistant could diagnose and prescribe a

remedy for a patient's disease (much like Edgar Cayce, who lived a couple of generations later).

Quimby built up a successful practice this way, but soon he came to a startling conclusion: it didn't matter what remedy was prescribed; it was the faith of the patient that made the difference. So Quimby dismissed his assistant and began to practice his own radical method of healing, in which he would simply convince the patient that he or she was already well. Quimby's warm and gentle nature aroused a sense of confidence. His office filled with patients, and many came away from his treatments feeling great relief or even fully cured. He often treated people for free when they could not pay.

A self-taught man, Quimby was not a systematic thinker. But around 1859, he began to formulate his teachings in writing. He believed he had discovered the secret of the miracles performed by Jesus Christ, and he wished to make this knowledge available to all. "My philosophy," he said, "will make man free and independent of all creeds and laws of man, and subject him to his own agreement, he being free from the laws of sin, sickness, and death."

The teaching was simple. In each human being resides Truth, Wisdom, and Goodness. This is our natural birthright. But there is also another aspect: the mortal, material mind that is subject to error. And the chief error to which this material mind is subject is disease. "Disease," Quimby wrote, "is false reasoning. True scientific wisdom is health and happiness. False reasoning is sickness and death." Quimby never really gave a name to his teaching, though he usually called it the "Science of Health." Once or twice in his writings he referred to it as "Christian Science."

Quimby attracted a number of disciples. One of them, Warren Felt Evans, was also a follower of the Swedish visionary Emanuel Swedenborg (1688–1772). It was in fact Evans who introduced the term "New Age" in his influential 1864 book, *The New Age and Its Messenger*. The "messenger" of the title was Swedenborg, who in his voluminous writings proclaimed 1757 as the year of the Last Judgment. But this event, he said, did not and was not supposed to take place on earth. It was enacted in the realm of the spirits, an intermediate zone between heaven and hell. The Lord purged this realm of evil, making it possible for heaven to transmit its influences to earth in a less impeded fashion. Swedenborg did not espouse the doctrine of thought power as it would later emerge: he held that the human mind was continually subject to influences from both heaven and hell and that the function of the human being on earth was to choose the good and renounce the evil impulses. Even so, Swedenborg's theology, which reached the zenith of its influence in the early nineteenth century, prepared the ground for the New Age movement.

After Quimby's death in 1866, his ideas lived on in the teachings of his most famous pupil, Mary Baker Eddy, who popularized the name "Christian Science" and created a religion around it, as well as in subsequent movements such as New Thought, Unity, and Religious Science.

New Thought is something of a blanket term used to cover these other movements in contradistinction to Eddy's Christian Science. The American scholar of religions Charles Braden characterized the chief differences between these two strains as follows: (1) Christian Scientists tend to be more authoritarian in their thinking, regarding Mrs. Eddy's writings as definitive revelations, whereas adherents of New Thought stress that spiritual truths are being revealed every day; (2) Christian Scientists have tended toward denial—disease, matter, and "mortal mind" do not exist—whereas the New Thought movement has inclined more toward affirmations ("I am well"; "I am perfect"); (3) Christian Scientists are generally opposed to working with traditional physicians or allowing their patients to do so, whereas proponents of New Thought have been more flexible and pragmatic on this count.[1]

One of the more vibrant strains of New Thought in the twentieth century was Religious Science, founded by

---

[1]Quoted in Gail Thain Parker, *Mind Cure in New England from the Civil War to World War I* (Hanover, N.H.: University Press of New England, 1973), 4–5.

Ernest Holmes (1887–1960). Born in Maine, as a teenager Holmes moved to Boston, where he took a two-year course in public speaking. At this time he was drawn to the works of Ralph Waldo Emerson (another major influence on the New Thought movement), as well as to Eddy's textbook of Christian Science, *Science and Health with Key to the Scriptures.* Later he would study other major figures in the New Thought movement, such as William Walker Atkinson and Thomas Troward.

In 1914, Holmes moved to Venice, California. In 1919, he published his first book, *Creative Mind.* His magnum opus, *Science of Mind,* was first published in 1926. Though most of Holmes's ideas can be found in his nineteenth-century precursors, he offered a slicker version of New Thought in his thoroughly twentieth-century salesmanship. He liked to tell stories of persuading homely girls to smile; when their lips parted, he claimed, they were surrounded by rich men eager to pay the bills for orthodontia. Gail Thain Parker, a scholar of New Thought, writes, "Holmes's smugness is very different from the more exploratory (and sometimes evasive) tone of the first- and second-generation mind curists. . . . He knew that nothing he would say would shock or surprise; his prose was full of lifetime warranties and unbeatable bargains."[2]

[2]Parker, 16–17.

Holmes, a powerful speaker but an ambivalent guru, nevertheless suffered his disciples to set up an organization to promote his ideas. The Institute of Religious Science and the School of Philosophy was incorporated in 1927. In the same year, Holmes also founded *Science of Mind* magazine, which is still published today. His influence was enormous, not only through his own writings but through those who were inspired by him. Norman Vincent Peale, author of *The Power of Positive Thinking*, a best-seller of the mid-twentieth century, drew much of his message from Religious Science.

Holmes lived long enough to see his organization subject to schisms and infighting. Shortly before Holmes's death, his protégé Obadiah Harris (who went on to become head of the Philosophical Research Society in Los Angeles) confided to him that he was leaving the movement to find his own path. "I wish I could go with you," Holmes replied.[3]

Even so, Holmes's organization survives to this day, and his teachings continue to inspire many. One of his central—and perhaps his most influential—ideas is the Law of Attraction. The term was originally coined in the nineteenth century to refer to the soul's affinity for

---

[3]Mitch Horowitz, *Occult America: The Secret History of How Mysticism Shaped Our Nation* (New York: Bantam, 2009), 97.

different spheres of the afterlife, but Holmes gave it its current meaning: "What we shall attract will depend on that on which our thoughts dwell."[4] If you think of prosperity, prosperity will come your way; if your thoughts dwell on disease, suffering, and misfortune, you are laying the ground for your own future unhappiness. These thoughts are not necessarily conscious ones, Holmes contended:

> While most disease must first have a subjective cause, this subjective cause (nine times out of ten) is not conscious in the thought of the person who suffers from it, but is perhaps largely the result of certain combinations of thinking. So while it is true that disease has its prototype in subjective mind, it is also true that the individual who suffers from the disease, frequently has never *thought* he was going to have that particular kind of trouble. But this does not alter the fact that every disease which comes up through subjectivity, and appears in the body, *must come through mind.*[5]

---

[4]Ernest Holmes, *The Science of Mind*, rev. ed. (New York: Tarcher/Penguin, 1998), 294.
[5]Holmes, 201–2; emphasis and capitalization here and in other quotes are from the original.

Healing, by contrast, comes from right thinking, as Quimby had taught decades before. Holmes taught his followers to heal in this way:

> First recognize your own perfection, then build up the same recognition for your patient. You are then ready to directly attack the *thought* that binds him, *recognizing that your word destroys it, and stating that it does*. You may then take into account and specifically mention everything that needs to be changed, every so-called broken law or false thought. Then finish your treatment with a realization of peace, remaining for a few moments in silent recognition that *your work is done, complete and perfect*.[6]

Holmes said that the human mind was composed of two aspects: the "subjective" or "subconscious" mind on the one hand, and the "objective" or "conscious" mind on the other. The subjective mind is not conscious but is creative; it is "that part of the mind which is set in motion as a creative thing in the conscious state." The subjective "sets power in motion in accordance with the thought."[7]

---

[6] Holmes, 202.
[7] Holmes, 30.

The conscious mind must, however, direct the subconscious toward positive goals.

A similar view can be found in the writings of Max Freedom Long, who, in such books as *The Secret Science Behind Miracles*, taught an almost identical system that he traced back to the kahunas, the shamans of Hawaii. According to Long, the Hawaiians used the word *"unihipili"* to describe what Holmes called the "subjective mind" and the word *"uhane"* as more or less equivalent to Holmes's "conscious" or "objective mind." Although both authors use the word "science" in a metaphysical context, it is unlikely that Holmes or Long influenced each other; rather these similarities show how thoroughly these ideas pervaded the alternative spirituality of early twentieth-century America.

By contrast, a work called *The Kybalion*, first published in 1908, was a likely influence on Holmes. The title page of this anonymous work lists its authors merely as "Three Initiates." The Chicago occultist William Walker Atkinson is generally acknowledged to have been one of these; Paul Foster Case, founder of the occult order known as Builders of the Adytum, is also sometimes suggested as one of the others.[8] In any event, *The Kybalion*—its name

------

[8] Horowitz, 210. Horowitz, however, believes that Atkinson was the sole author.

allegedly going back to the Egyptian mysteries, although its meaning was supposedly lost—set forth seven principles of metaphysical truth, the first being "the principle of mentalism"—"THE UNIVERSE IS MENTAL—HELD IN THE MIND OF THE ALL. . . . THE UNIVERSE, AND ALL IT CONTAINS, IS A MENTAL CREATION OF THE ALL."[9] Compare this to Holmes's statement "THERE IS ONE MENTAL LAW IN THE UNIVERSE, AND WHERE WE USE IT, IT BECOMES OUR LAW BECAUSE WE HAVE INDIVIDUALIZED IT."[10] (The similarities extend to the printing of both sentences in all capital letters.)

Since the universe was "mental" in its essence, Holmes prescribed what today is called "creative visualization" as a means of attaining well-being. Here is his advice to someone who is seeking success in business:

Every day he should see his place filled with people. See them looking at and finding pleasure in his merchandise; see them comparing prices and realizing that he is offering good values; see them delighted with the service he is giving. . . . Make a mental picture of it all. We are dealing with Intelligence, and we should recognize the Power we are

[9]"Three Initiates," *The Kybalion* (Clayton, Ga.: Tri-State Press, 1988 [1908]), 53, 57.
[10]Holmes, 30.

working with—realizing our Oneness with it—and then we should ask for what we wish and take it.[11]

A related approach is *affirmation*. Like the ancient Semites, who believed in a mystical unity between a word and the thing it represented, Holmes believed that the spoken word held the power to transform reality, and he included affirmations as part of his prescribed practice. He recommended making this statement, for example, as part of a "treatment" for "supply": "I always have an abundance of money and an abundance of whatever it takes to make life happy and opulent. There is a continuous movement toward me of supply, of money, of all that I need to express the fullest life, happiness and action."[12]

Even this brief account gives a reasonably clear idea of Holmes's Science of Mind and the worldview that it entails. Anthropologists have classically distinguished between *magic* and *religion*. Magic uses certain techniques such as incantation, sacrifice, and ritual as a way of manipulating unseen powers. Religion often uses the same methods but it does so as a way of supplicating God or the gods through prayer and meditation. Magic is a kind of sacred technology, while religion usually involves a relationship

[11]Holmes, 300.
[12]Holmes, 263.

to a personal deity. Science of Mind—and the religion of positive thinking as a whole—is much closer to magic than to religion. While it does not prescribe arcane rituals or weird spells, it does attempt to manipulate the primordial force of the universe—mind—on the practitioner's behalf. There is no theological problem in this from a New Thought perspective, because God is all-good and all-loving and wants us to live in health and abundance; our failure to do so is simply the result of faulty thinking and a failure to claim our due. The constant use of the word "science" by figures from Quimby to Holmes underlines the quasi-technological mindset that operates in these teachings, and suggests how much they owe to the industrial age that gave them birth: mind is an impersonal force that can be harnessed in much the same way as steam or electricity.

While New Thought and Religious Science insist that they are part of a tradition that has always been known to adepts—the healing miracles of Jesus are frequently cited as cases in point—there is comparatively little in traditional esotericism that resembles these teachings. Certainly it has long been taught, particularly by Plato and his philosophical descendants, that there is an ideal world of forms that can be perceived by the higher intellect and that serve as prototypes for the things of materiality. But the teaching that someone can not only perceive these archetypes but manipulate them to change physical reality is rare. The traditional view was that a true philosopher did not care about the material world and occupied himself as little as possible with it.

Even the occultism of the Renaissance, with its cumbrous magical technology, did not lay any particular emphasis upon thought power. According to Renaissance savants such as Paracelsus and Cornelius Agrippa, the magus *can* affect the higher dimensions, but does so by operating upon their corresponding objects in the physical world. To bring down beneficent solar or jovial influences, one wears stones or eats herbs that are associated with these benign influences. Magical formulae were also employed, but not as affirmations—many of these incantations consist of words in no known language—and the goal was often to subject spirits and demons to the magician's will.

The world of traditional magic is thus very far removed from the streamlined positive thoughts and affirmations of Religious Science and its kin. To speculate wildly for a moment, perhaps this is one sign of the New Age proclaimed by Swedenborg and Evans—that what formerly required intricate spells and bizarre operations can now be accomplished by using the power of the mind and the spoken word.

This, of course, assumes that the methods of Religious Science actually work, and such claims are hard to assess.

Certainly there are any number of people who have been willing to testify on behalf of these procedures, and their claims must be taken seriously enough. But we have no way of knowing how many of them there are as opposed to the numbers of those who have tried and failed. Most of the people I have known through New Thought circles appear no richer, happier, healthier, or more successful than much of the rest of humanity. And while I have known people who have gotten rich over the years—some of them staggeringly rich—their secret was probably not affirmations or thought power but the usual combination of talent, hard work, and sheer luck—and, indeed, enormous quantities of all three.

Nonetheless, the claims of the thought power gurus from Quimby to Holmes (not to mention latter-day figures such as the entity known as Abraham, channeled by Esther Hicks, and Rhonda Byrne, author of *The Secret*) cannot be dismissed wholesale. Thought power, like so many aspects of the metaphysical realm, occupies a liminal space between truth and falsity. As soon as you have decided it is all nonsense, something pokes you on the shoulder and tells you it may not be nonsense after all. But if you become an enthusiastic believer, you may end up disappointed.

To speak personally, I would be willing to say this much. The basic idea behind positive thinking is true: there is a mental world that underlays the physical, and thoughts can influence events in ways that can seem bizarre or even paranormal. But the interplay of thought and actuality is not entirely explained by a few simplistic axioms and the usual lifetime warranties. Other factors operate as well—the obscure but overwhelming forces that are sometimes called fate and destiny; the actions of a mind that cannot always be understood, much less manipulated, by the conscious ego; and of course the "time and chance" that, the Bible reminds us, "happeneth to all" (Eccles. 9:11).

To the extent that positive thinking and mental science help us focus upon our goals and eliminate negative mental patterns, they can be useful. But they are usually not very effective substitutes for action. And if they foster a self-centered attitude that focuses on "my" prosperity and "my" health, or, still worse, dismisses the suffering of others on the grounds that somehow they brought it all upon themselves by wrong thinking, these ideas can cause serious trouble. We must never lose sight of the fact that the power of thought includes the power to enslave the mind. And the ultimate goal of liberation may not be to make our thoughts manifest in the world of desire, but to free ourselves from them as much as possible.

## Thirteen

# THE MYSTERIOUS
## *KYBALION*

PEOPLE WHO HAVE SPENT TIME grazing in metaphysical bookshops may have come across a mysterious volume called *The Kybalion*, written by "Three Initiates" and
first issued by the Yogi Publication Society of Chicago in
1908. The most familiar edition is a plain volume bound in
blue cloth and stamped with gold, in a format like those of
other books from the same publisher, including various
works on yoga by one Swami Ramacharaka.

*The Kybalion* claims to be a brief introduction to a mystical tradition that has survived from antiquity. The core
of the work is a series of aphorisms that, the authors contend, go back to the "early days" and were "passed on from
teacher to student, . . . the exact signification and meaning
of the terms having been lost for several centuries." The
word, taken at face value, looks vaguely Greek, but it has
no meaning in this language (the closest Greek word to it,

curiously, is *kybeia*, meaning "dice game" or "trickery"). It is also tempting to connect this work with the Jewish mystical tradition known as the Kabbalah, but as a matter of fact the Kabbalah is never mentioned in *The Kybalion*. Rather it presents itself as the essence of the teaching of Hermes Trismegistus ("Thrice-Greatest Hermes"), a legendary, semidivine figure who is said to have brought learning to Egypt in the remotest past. Hermes Trismegistus is often identified both with the Greek god Hermes and the Egyptian god Thoth.

*The Kybalion* is organized according to seven basic principles, which, it says, form the basis of occult philosophy:

1. MENTALISM. "The All is Mind; the Universe is mental."

2. CORRESPONDENCE. "As above, so below; as below, so above."

3. VIBRATION. "Nothing rests; everything moves; everything vibrates."

4. POLARITY. "Everything is Dual; everything has poles; everything has its pair of opposites."

5. RHYTHM. "Everything flows, out and in; everything has its tides; all things rise and fall."

6. CAUSE AND EFFECT. "Every Cause has its Effect; every Effect has its Cause; everything happens according to Law."

7. GENDER. "Gender is in everything; everything has its Masculine and Feminine Principles; Gender manifests on all planes."

The origins of this book are difficult to trace. As I noted in the previous chapter, "The Science of Thought," it is believed to have been written by William Walker Atkinson, who operated the Yogi Publication Society in Chicago (he is generally acknowledged to be "Swami Ramacharaka"). As the first principle—"Mentalism"—suggests, the ideas of *The Kybalion* bear some resemblance to New Thought, a movement to which Atkinson was closely connected. The universe, *The Kybalion* tells us, is contained in "the Mind of the All": "The All creates the Universe mentally, in a manner akin to the process whereby Man creates Mental Images." This idea is central to practically all New Thought teachings. Nevertheless, the book does echo a more remote past. The term "The All," for example, resembles the Greek *to pan*—which also means "the all" and which appears in some Hermetic maxims, most famously *Hen to pan*: "All is one."

Given the claims made for it, the most obvious source to examine for the roots of *The Kybalion* is the *Corpus Her-*

*meticum* or "Hermetic body" of texts. These were composed in the early centuries A.D. and purport to expound the wisdom of Egypt as narrated in a series of discourses and dialogues including Hermes and his son Tat (a version of "Thoth"). And indeed there are intriguing resemblances between these works and *The Kybalion*. The first text of the *Corpus Hermeticum*, the *Poimandres* (whose name is probably a Greek adaptation of the Egyptian *p-eime-n-re* or "mind of authority"), tells us that the source of the universe was *nous*—consciousness or mind—much as *The Kybalion* asserts the principle of "Mentalism." Moreover, this divine mind is described as "being androgyne and existing as light and life"—which parallels the concept of "Gender" as set out in *The Kybalion*.

*The Kybalion* also speaks of the principle of correspondence. This idea appears in another ancient Hermetic text: the extremely brief and elliptical *Emerald Tablet*, which says, *"Quod est superius est sicut quod est inferius, et quod est inferius est sicut quod est superius, ad perpetranda miracula rei unius"*: "What is above is like what is below, and what is below is like what is above, to enact the wonders of the one thing." (The *Emerald Tablet* is said to have originally been written in Syriac, a Semitic language spoken in antiquity in the eastern Mediterranean world, but it survives only in somewhat dissimilar versions in Latin and Arabic.)

Whether there really was a collection of aphorisms

known as *The Kybalion* that was passed down from master to pupil from ancient times is hard to say. There are, to my knowledge, no copies of it in any form that predate the 1908 edition, but that does not mean there were none. And there are claims of similarly hidden texts in other traditions. The Russian esotericist Boris Mouravieff claimed that esoteric Christianity has an unpublished set of aphorisms called *The Golden Book*, some of which he quotes in his three-volume work *Gnosis: Study and Commentaries on the Esoteric Tradition of Eastern Orthodoxy* (although these do not resemble the maxims of *The Kybalion* to any great degree).

In a blog posting, Tarot scholar Mary K. Greer suggests a plausible direct source for *The Kybalion*. In 1884, Anna Kingsford, an Englishwoman who founded an organization called the Hermetic Society, published a book entitled *The Virgin of the World of Hermes Trismegistus*, which presents an adaptation of the Hermetic texts. And in fact the introduction to *The Virgin of the World*, written by Kingsford's associate Edward Maitland, does contain a number of things that are echoed in *The Kybalion*. For example, Maitland asserts that consciousness is "the indispensable condition of existence," and that matter "is a mode of consciousness," which certainly resonates with *The Kybalion*'s doctrine of mentalism. Maitland also mentions "the law of correspondence between all planes, or spheres, of existence." He also speaks of "the doctrine of Karma," which dictates "the impossibility either of getting good by doing evil, or of escaping the penalty of the latter"—an obvious parallel to *The Kybalion*'s "law of cause and effect." In light of these resemblances and *The Kybalion*'s insistence that it contains the essence of Hermetic teaching, it is very likely that Kingsford and Maitland's work was at least one of *The Kybalion*'s sources.

Thus it is possible to trace out a lineage for *The Kybalion*: the original Hermetic texts, which have been known in the Western world since the fifteenth century and which have existed in English versions since at least the seventeenth; and the digest of these texts as presented by Kingsford and Maitland in Victorian London.

But there is a major difference between the original Hermetic teachings and the New Thought–flavored doctrines of *The Kybalion*. The *Corpus Hermeticum* did not exist in a philosophical vacuum; its elevated and abstruse dialogues form only a part of the ancient Hermetic literature. Much of the rest consists of magical texts, and scholars have become increasingly aware that these cannot be so easily divorced in content or inspiration from the Hermetic writings.

In short, the ancient Hermetists probably did not use a type of New Thought–like mind power in their practice. Rather they probably made use of such things as magical rituals, divination, and invocations of the gods, just as we see in most ancient religions. The use of mind power as we find it in New Thought seems to be very much an innovation of the nineteenth century.

Hence the aphorisms in *The Kybalion* are very likely a pious fraud. Certainly their style and mode of thought are more evocative of twentieth-century America than of ancient Egypt or Greece. Even so, it would be mistaken to conclude that this work is unfaithful to the tradition it invokes. A spiritual tradition is based, certainly, on timeless and unchanging truths; but the application to which these truths are put will vary from age to age, in accordance with that age's need. In this sense, *The Kybalion* can lay genuine claim to the Hermetic heritage.

## SOURCES

Copenhaver, Brian P. *Hermetica: The Greek* Corpus Hermeticum *and the Latin Asclepius in a New English Translation with Notes and an Introduction.* Cambridge: Cambridge University Press, 1992.

Greer, Mary K. "Sources of *The Kybalion* in Anna Kingsford's Hermetic System": http://marygreer.wordpress.com/2009/10/08/source-of-the-kybalion-in-anna-kingsford%E2%80%99s-hermetic-system; accessed Nov. 11, 2010.

Kingsford, Anna, and Edward Maitland. *The Virgin of the World of Hermes Mercurius Trismegistus*: http://www.sacred-texts.com/eso/vow/index.htm; accessed Nov. 11, 2010.

Scott, Walter. *Hermetica: The Ancient Greek and Latin Writings Which Contain Religious or Philosophic Teachings Ascribed to Hermes Trismegistus.* Boston: Shambhala, 1985 [1924].

"Three Initiates." *The Kybalion.* Clayton, Ga.: Tri-State Press, 1988 [1908].

Van den Broek, Roelof. "Hermetic Literature I: Antiquity." In Wouter J. Hanegraaff et al., eds., *Dictionary of Gnosis and Western Esotericism* (Leiden: Brill, 2005), 1:487–99.

# Fourteen

## DEMONS AMONG US

WHEN I WAS A BOY, I remember reading an account by popular occult writer Frank Edwards entitled "He Conjured Up a Demon That Killed Him!" I don't remember the details of this story, largely because I was too terrified to read it more than once. But the question remains: do demons exist? If so, what are they and what is their relationship with us?

The skeptical materialist will reply automatically that of course demons don't exist: they are merely figments of the imagination. Unfortunately, this response says nothing. All sorts of things are figments of the human imagination, ranging from great artistic visions to perverted political philosophies that have started world wars. Such figments have very real and palpable consequences, so to dismiss them on the grounds that they are imaginary proves nothing. The demons conjured up by the twentieth-century imagination killed not one lone occultist but hundreds of millions of people around the world.

According to modern psychiatry, people who see or hear demons are usually suffering from some kind of neurochemical imbalance that causes them to perceive things that are not really there. No doubt this is often the case—but does that mean that all experiences of this kind are due to neurochemical imbalances, particularly when they occur to people who are otherwise normal and functional? Again, a reductionistic answer explains nothing. It is not an answer but the avoidance of an answer.

A more sophisticated approach appears in the work of the Swiss psychologist C. G. Jung and his school. According to Jung, these demons and other unseen entities have a reality, but it is a psychic reality. They represent aspects of the self that the conscious ego cannot accept and has relegated to the darkness of the unconscious. The Jungian analyst Alfred Ribi writes:

> The psyche is whole only in a relative sense. It is comprised of fragmentary personalities, among which the ego personality is only one of many, though it is a central personality. The other fragmentary personalities are either incompatible with the ego or not yet suited for consciousness.... As individual tendencies cross the threshold of con-

sciousness, they are represented in consciousness and can be selected by consciousness as suitable for total functioning. Whatever does not fit is immediately repressed, that is, pushed down into the unconscious. There it stays until, through further repressions of related material, it becomes sufficiently charged with energy to penetrate into consciousness as a disturbance.[1]

The amount of energy needed by these repressed parts of the psyche in order to make their presence felt varies with circumstances. When the conscious ego begins to doze on its watch—a phenomenon Jung called *abaissement du niveau mental*, or "lowering of the mental level"—the demons resurface. This most commonly happens during sleep. Most people can identify with Job when he cries, "Thou scarest me with dreams, and terrifiest me through visions" (Job 7:14). But fatigue, exhaustion, acute stress, or anguish can also lower one's mental level, allowing these repressed elements to come to awareness. Or, as Ribi suggests above, they will break through willy-nilly when they have accumulated enough power.

The Jungian view, as Ribi emphasizes, is that "the

---

[1] Alfred Ribi, *Demons of the Inner World: Understanding Our Hidden Complexes*, trans. Michael H. Kohn (Boston: Shambhala, 1990), 142–43.

psyche is whole only in a relative sense." There are all sorts of material in our minds that our conscious mind cannot accept—usually because they conflict with the ego's self-image. A man who considers himself mild-mannered will not be able to acknowledge the violence within him. Yet the capacity for violence remains the common legacy of the human race. While it may be stronger in some people than others, it is rarely absent from anyone. Thus it behooves a person—particularly one who is on the path of greater self-awareness—to acknowledge these elements in himself. Jung referred to these semiautonomous aspects of the psyche as "complexes"; but in many cases they are almost indistinguishable from what the old occult traditions called "demons."

Does conscious awareness of these darker aspects of your own nature make them go away? Sometimes. The twentieth-century spiritual master G. I. Gurdjieff said:

By observing himself [a man] throws, as it were, a ray of light onto his inner processes which have hitherto worked in complete darkness. And under the influence of this light the processes themselves begin to change. There are a great many chemical processes that can take place only in the absence of light. Exactly in the same way many psychic processes can take place only in the dark. Even a feeble

light of consciousness is enough to change completely the character of a process, while it makes
many of them altogether impossible.[2]

This is undoubtedly true in many circumstances. Seeing
your own inner demons—the fragments of lust, hatred,
greed, envy, and so on—that lurk in your psyche will at
the very least change your relationship with them. They
will be comparatively available to the conscious mind,
which will then have a better chance of forestalling their
worst manifestations. If you know where your anger is in
yourself, so to speak, you have that much better a chance
of preventing it from bursting out at the wrong times. If
you can see your own lust, you are more likely to keep it
from sabotaging your relationships or making a fool out of
you. But it would be extremely simplistic to say that mere
awareness will dissipate your inner demons in every case.

The process of integration of these elements—Jung
called it "individuation"—is a long and usually painful
one. Jung's principal technique to this end is called "active
imagination." Essentially the patient goes to the analyst
and describes a recent dream that seemed significant.
Inevitably there are other characters in this dream besides

---

[2]In P. D. Ouspensky, *In Search of the Miraculous: Fragments of a Forgotten Teaching* (New York: Harcourt, Brace, 1950), 146.

the dreamer. Active imagination usually involves pretending that one or more of these dream characters is present in the room and having a conversation with you. Gradually, as a result of this interaction, these figures will transform themselves or disappear. Jung, in the chapter of his biography *Memories, Dreams, Reflections* entitled "Confrontation with the Unconscious," describes his own experiences with this technique.

The most significant of the inner figures he encountered was a wise man named Philemon.

Philemon was a pagan and brought with him an Egypto-Hellenistic atmosphere with a Gnostic coloration. . . . Philemon and other figures of my fantasies brought home to me the crucial insight that there are things in the psyche which I do not produce, but which produce themselves and have their own life. Philemon represented a force which was not myself. In my fantasies I held conversations with him, and he said things which I had not consciously thought. For I observed clearly that it was he who spoke, not I. He said I treated thoughts as if I generated them myself, but in his view thoughts were like animals in the forest, or people in a room, or birds in the air, and added, "If you should see people in a room, you would not think that you had made those people, or that you were responsible for them." It was he who taught me psychic objectivity, the reality of the psyche.[3]

These observations possess a subtlety that is often lost in many treatments of Jung's thought, even by some of his disciples. Up to a point it is no doubt true that the demons you struggle with—as well as the wise spirits that will educate you—are disowned fragments of the psyche. But are they really the creation of *you*, the individual who was born on a specific date and lives in such-and-such a place? As Jung saw, this can by no means be taken for granted. Right after discussing Philemon in his autobiography, he goes on to tell of an Indian he knew, a friend of Gandhi's, who claimed that his guru was Shankaracharya, the great exponent of the Advaita Vedanta who lived around the eighth century A.D. "There are ghostly gurus too," the Indian told him. "Most people have living gurus. But there are always some who have a spirit for a teacher." Similarly, my friend Warren Kenton, the British Kabbalist who writes under the name Z'ev ben Shimon Halevi, has told me that he has been taught by Ibn Gabirol, a Jewish philosopher of the eleventh century A.D.

---

[3]C. G. Jung, *Memories, Dreams, Reflections*, trans. Richard and Clara Winston (New York: Vintage, 1989), 182–83.

In short, there is something inimitably *other* about many of the spirits and demons that one encounters, whether as a result of inner work or merely fortuitously. I can remember an instance that occurred twenty-five years ago. I was asleep alone in my bed and having an ordinary dream (about what I do not remember). Suddenly and quite intrusively, a kind of demon, of a slimy greenish color, intruded into the dream—or rather intruded into me as I was having the dream. I felt a kind of physical collision with this entity, and the shock sent me hurtling back into my body from wherever I had been traveling in the psychic realms. I was shaken and frightened, but was not harmed in any discernible way, and life was normal the next day.

This experience (and others like it) leads me to distinguish between dream figures, figures that are generated in one's own psyche, and other things that are not part of oneself at any level but attempt to intrude into the self. As alarming as my experience was, I had to look back on it and say that in reality it is nothing more than happens all the time in the physical world. After all, the body is constantly fighting off microbes and parasites and usually does the job quite well as long as it is functioning normally. I had to draw a similar conclusion about this experience. A kind of psychic parasite had attempted to get in, and my normal defense mechanisms fought it off more or less automatically.

Struggles with demons have long been a part of mystical literature. One of the most famous cases is that of St. Anthony (or Antony) the Hermit, the third-century founder of Christian monasticism. The Church Father Athanasius, in his classic biography of Anthony, writes:

> The devil, unhappy wight, one night even took upon him the shape of a woman and imitated all her acts simply to beguile Antony. But he, his mind filled with Christ and the nobility inspired by Him, and considering the spirituality of the soul, quenched the coal of the other's deceit. Again the enemy suggested the ease of pleasure. But he like a man filled with rage and grief turned his thoughts to the threatened fire and the gnawing worm, and setting these in array against his adversary, passed through the temptation unscathed. All this was a source of shame to his foe.[4]

For centuries, Anthony's struggles with his devils have inspired artists from Hieronymus Bosch to Gustave Flaubert, who wrote a novel entitled *The Temptation of St. Anthony*.

---

[4]Athanasius of Alexandria, *Life of St. Antony*, trans. H. Ellershaw: http://www .fordham.edu/halsall/basis/VITA-ANTONY.html; accessed July 8, 2009, 15.

As fascinating as all this may be, we seem to have come full circle in our inquiry. Jung spoke of integrating these elements of the psyche; but for Anthony and most of the Christian mystics who followed in his wake, the devil is not to be integrated but to be opposed and fought. The stance one takes toward these entities, which are so much loathed and feared, depends upon the metaphysical status you accord them. Do you take them as genuine, independent entities, as Christianity and most traditional religions have done, or do you regard them as mere shards of the psyche?

This question is hard to answer for one principal reason: psychic entities are, by definition, not physical. Conventional thought, on the other hand, assigns identity on the basis of physical criteria: the reason that you are not me is that we have different bodies. How do we make this determination for a realm where there are no bodies in any familiar sense of that word?

Contemporary philosophy and psychology are thus highly skeptical about the independent existence of spirits and demons. On the other hand, these disciplines do not understand the psyche very well. They have no coherent, generally accepted vision of how the mind works, what its pieces are, or what holds it together. I suspect that psychology is at the same state surgery was in, say, 1600, before William Harvey had created an accurate model of the circulation of the blood. And if you have no clear picture of what a mind is, how are you going to tell where one mind starts and another one stops?

The esoteric traditions answer this question by saying that we do indeed have bodies apart from the physical. A body in this sense is a structure for organizing experience at a certain level. The physical body is the structure through which we collect and organize physical experience. Subtler bodies are structures for organizing experience at other levels. The best known of these, the astral body, is the means for organizing psychic—that is to say, psychological—experience as a whole. It overlaps with the physical body but can be detached from it under certain circumstances. Many occultists say that the dream world is a reality in which the astral body travels while the physical body sleeps. If we go back and look at my dream encounter above, we might suppose that my semidetached astral body collided with that of a demonic—that is to say, potentially harmful—entity, and the shock led it to reconnect immediately with my physical form.

If, of course, I had not been in reasonably good physical and psychological health, this entity might have gotten in and caused trouble. Over the years I have met people who were psychologically disturbed and who said that they were in contact with spirit entities. Once, when I was editor of *Gnosis*, a journal of the Western inner traditions, I received a call out of the blue from a woman in Australia (which was itself rather remarkable in that *Gnosis* was published out of San Francisco). She insisted that the Gnostic demiurge Yahweh (as she called it) was tormenting and assaulting her—which she said was happening even as we were talking. Although I felt sorry for her, there was not much I could do except talk to her for a while and suggest that she tell the entity to go away (this works comparatively often). In the end I gave her the number of a crisis line for spiritual emergencies. Possibly she was schizophrenic—or is what we call schizophrenia at least partly the result of psychic intrusions of this kind?

Some of the entities that we call demons are undoubtedly disowned parts of the self. Others seem to exist autonomously, and indeed traditional knowledge insists that the world is full of such creatures. Samuel Taylor Coleridge, in an annotation to his own poem *The Rime of the Ancient Mariner*, mentions "the invisible inhabitants of this planet, neither departed souls nor angels; concerning whom the learned Jew, Josephus, and the Platonic Constantinopolitan, Michael Psellus, may be consulted. They are very numerous, and there is no climate or element without one or more of them."[5] I do not think that Coleridge was merely indulging his poetic imagination here. Traditional

---

[5] Samuel Taylor Coleridge, *The Rime of the Ancient Mariner*, part 2.

knowledge would add that some of these entities are benevolent toward humanity, while others harbor nothing but hostile intentions. Still others are neutral or simply unaware of us, as we usually are of them.

Up to now we have been speaking of these spirit entities as having an organic existence: they are life forms as we are and are part of the invisible, but still natural, ecology. But the esoteric tradition speaks of another class of beings that are not "invisible inhabitants of this planet" but the creations of the human mind. There is even a name for them: "egregores," derived from the Greek γρηγορεω (grēgoreo), "to watch."

To understand what they are, we need to go back to basic occult theory. Any thought or image created in the mind has a certain existence in the astral realm. The vast majority of these, like most of our thoughts, have no independent life; they rise and fall like sparks from a smith's hammer. But if, for whatever purpose, one focuses on a thought and directs mental energy toward it, it begins to grow in power. After a tremendous amount of such investment, it can even appear to be quasi-autonomous, having a life and purpose of its own. Whether it really does or not is moot; but to all intents and purposes it can act like a spirit, and a powerful one.

The strength of such an entity is multiplied if many people concentrate their attention on it. The great Christian esotericist Valentin Tomberg, author of *Meditations on the Tarot*, contended that the gods worshipped by the ancient Canaanites—Baal, Moloch, Astarte—were just such egregores. We can go a step further and ask ourselves whether our familiar Devil is the nearly omnipotent fallen angel that Christianity portrays or is rather the collective creation of millions of Christians over the centuries who have directed psychic energy (chiefly in the form of fear) toward this image of the Devil and unwittingly given it life. Whatever conclusion one may reach, one is not likely to find the answer reassuring.

If a nation or people can create an egregore, can it become possessed by one in turn? If one credits Tomberg, this is precisely what happened to the ancient Canaanite races—at least according to their enemies the Israelites, whose accounts are our chief sources of information.

Jung, in a 1936 essay entitled "Wotan," argued that the Germany of his time had become possessed by a resurgent archetype in the national, or, if you like, racial psyche: the ancient Germanic god Wotan, "a restless wanderer who creates unrest and stirs up strife."[6] But was this really the old god Wotan or an egregore created by the anxieties and longings of the German nation?

---

[6]In C. G. Jung, *Civilization in Transition*, trans. R. F. C. Hull (New York: Pantheon/Bollingen, 1964), 180.

One man who was probably possessed in this way was Adolf Hitler, who wrote in a 1915 poem:

*I often go on bitter nights*
*To Wotan's oak in the quiet glade*
*With dark powers to weave a union—*
*The runic letter the moon makes with its magic spell*
*And all who are full of impudence during the day*
*Are made small by the magic formula!*[7]

This short poem recapitulates several salient themes in Hitler's life: the "union" with "dark powers"; the preoccupation with ancient Germanic myth; and, perhaps most important, the humiliation of those "who are full of impudence." According to one of Hitler's biographers, he adopted his characteristic hanging forelock and toothbrush moustache from a painting of Wotan that he had seen.[8] If Hitler really did awaken the sleeping god Wotan, he, like the magician in the Frank Edwards story, conjured up a demon that in the end killed him.

Hitler himself has turned into a kind of egregore since his demise, exacting veneration from extreme rightists and even some esotericists. The eccentric Chilean author

[7]Quoted in "Wotan," World Spirituality Web site: http://www.worldspirituality .org/wotan.html; accessed July 11, 2009.
[8]George Victor, *Hitler: The Pathology of Evil* (Hendon, Va.: Potomac, 1999), 88.

and diplomat Miguel Serrano has issued a manifesto calling for the reincarnation of the Führer, "Last Avatar of Wotan."[9]

In any event, one thing is clear. There is such a thing as collective insanity—a type of dementia that overcomes entire peoples, leading to massacres and atrocities. What is particularly bizarre is that many of the people performing these evil deeds remain otherwise sane and functional, just as the commandants of the concentration camps went home in the evenings and listened to Bach and Mozart with their families. We can wonder whether the collective level of the psyche is like an internal organ, which can become diseased and dysfunctional while the rest of the body is healthy. Whatever we may conclude, it is the case that this type of madness exists; history is a witness to it. And yet it is unexplained or at best given pseudoexplanations in merely sociological or economical terms.

Are there dark entities floating in the astral realms, longing to prey upon humanity because, as with Frankenstein's monster, it is humanity that has created them? We do not know. The evidence would seem to suggest as much. At any rate, I am convinced that we will not understand

[9]Miguel Serrano, "Hitler and the Last Avatar": http://allfatherwotan.org /hitleravatar.html; accessed July 11, 2009.

the rise and fall of civilizations, or history itself, until we do know.

There is always the temptation, when considering such grim possibilities, of being overtaken by fear, of feeling suddenly surrounded by malignant forces of almost infinite might. This is not entirely warranted. Whatever powers these entities possess in their own realm, they require human acquiescence and cooperation in order to make themselves manifest. We can defeat them at a collective level by setting aside our own hatreds and fears, of which they are personifications. When confronting these dark forces individually, it is helpful to realize that it is we and not they that have the advantage. Even when they are not the creations of our own minds, the fact that humans have a physical form gives us access to a stability and power that purely psychic entities lack. Indeed their only chance for success is by luring us into forgetting this fact.

# Fifteen

# TOXIC PRAYER

You MIGHT BE UNDER THE impression that authors choose the titles of their own books. That isn't true—at least not always. If the publishers don't like the title, they will change it.

Such was the fate of a book published in 1997 by the noted mind-body researcher Larry Dossey, M.D., author of *Healing Words* and *Prayer Is Good Medicine*. Dossey had written on a provocative subject: if thoughts and prayers have the power to heal, do they also have the power to harm? He called his book *Toxic Prayer*, but the publishers, Harper San Francisco (now Harper One), were extremely uncomfortable with this title. They feared a backlash from fundamentalist Christians, who, they imagined, would take up arms against the idea that any kind of prayer could ever be harmful. After an anxious discussion that went all the way to the top of the company's hierarchy, another, safer, though more flavorless title was chosen: *Be Careful What You Pray For . . . You Might Just Get It.*

Whether the decision was a wise one or not (controversy sells books, after all), the whole story raises an awkward issue: is prayer a morally ambiguous force? Can it be used to curse as well as bless? If so, how?

Of course it depends upon what you mean by prayer. In the conventional monotheistic view, prayer is addressed to the one true God (or sometimes his subordinates, such as Mary or the saints or the angels). Since God is all-good, he will either grant this request if it is beneficial or ignore it if it isn't.

This belief, although engagingly simple and clear, begins to erode if we also accept the idea that thoughts have power in and of themselves. By this view, a thought, whether positive or negative or neutral, has effects that can be felt in the psychic dimension and sometimes physically as well. This perspective, which takes us out of the sphere of religion *per se* and into that of magic, provides a far more equivocal picture of prayer.

Magic, wrote the notorious twentieth-century occultist Aleister Crowley, is "the Science and Art of causing Change to occur in conformity with Will." This definition, while correct up to a point, is too general to be entirely adequate. If I move a coffee cup around my table with my hand, I am effecting change in conformity with will, but no one would claim that that is magic. Magic has to do with effecting change by *occult* means—that is, by means invisible to ordinary sight and inadmissible by ordinary consciousness. If I were to move the same coffee cup around the table without touching it, this would start to look like magic, since the cause of the movement, whatever it is, cannot be seen.

There are many forms of magic, ranging from sleight of hand (that is, using the standard tricks of stage magicians) to suggestion to more genuinely paranormal means. The boundaries between these categories—like the boundary between prayer and magic—are fluid and permeable, but generally we can say that occult magic is believed to work through two principal methods.

The first has to do with spirits. Most occultists believe that there are unseen creatures inhabiting dimensions of reality that intersect with our own: these beings are variously known as spirits, elementals, angels, demons, *devas*—the lore has countless names for them. According to the magical worldview, it's possible to engage with these creatures. The magicians of the Renaissance, for example, evoked certain spirits using occult rites. If these spirits were approached the right way (through seals, signs, rituals, invocations, and so on), it was believed that they could be beseeched or, more often, forced to obey the magician's will. The moral status of these spirits was ambiguous—they were often thought to be demons—but that could prove an advantage when there was dirty work to be done. Here is one invocation, of a spirit called Mirael. Taken from a fifteenth-century manuscript of necromancy found in Munich, it is designed to make someone lose his mind:

> May Mirael enter into your brain and dissolve and destroy all wisdom, sense, discretion, and thought. I conjure you, Mirael, by all the princes and elders, and by all that you wish to do, that for as long as it pleases me you will flow through the person I look upon and daze him, and that he lose everything that he does not recognize. Otherwise I shall cast you into the depths of the sea so that you shall not escape for eternity.

As unsavory as these practices may sound, they are universal or practically so. Here is another example, this one from the other end of the world. Max Freedom Long, the redoubtable investigator of the Hawaiian form of shamanism known as *huna*, discusses the death prayer as practiced by the shamans or kahunas: "To become able to use the 'death prayer' a kahuna had to inherit from another kahuna one or more ghostly subconscious spirits. (Or he might, if sufficiently psychic, locate subconscious spirits or ghosts, and use hypnotic suggestion to enslave or capture them.)" Once a kahuna had some of these spirits under his will, he would offer them food and drink so as to imbue them with "mana" or vital force and then give them very specific instructions about what to do with this energy. They might, for example, be told to find a given person and enter his body or attach themselves to it. Once they had done this, they would suck up the victim's vital force. When the victim died, the spirits would return to their master, further strengthened by having absorbed the dead person's mana.

Spirits thus require an infusion of energy or life force. There are a number of ways of supplying it. In ancient times the method of choice was blood sacrifice; as the victim's blood spilled, the vital force would, as it were, evaporate so that the spirits could consume it. Homer's Odysseus describes a sacrifice he has made: "When I had prayed sufficiently to the dead, I cut the throats of the two sheep and let the blood run into the trench, whereon the ghosts came trooping up from Erebus—brides, young bachelors, old men worn out with toil, maids who had been crossed in love, and brave men who had been killed in battle, with their armour still smirched with blood; they came from every quarter and flitted round the trench with a strange kind of screaming sound that made me turn pale with fear." While blood sacrifice is much less common today than it was in antiquity, it is still used, for example, in Santería, Voudun, and other religions of African origin that are practiced in the Caribbean Islands and South America.

To show how the death prayer works, Long tells of a young Irishman who went to Honolulu and worked as a taxi driver. He became involved with a Hawaiian girl, who then ended her engagement with a Hawaiian boy. The girl's grandmother, not trusting the young Irishman's intentions, tried to break up the affair, but without success.

One day, writes Long, the Irishman's feet "went to sleep." The pricking numbness that afflicted his feet gradually crept up his body, making him unable to move. The young man did not believe in magic or death prayers or any such nonsense, so he called in conventional American doctors. They were unable to help him. The numbness had spread to his waist by the time an old doctor who had practiced in the islands for many years was summoned. He recognized the symptoms of the death prayer and, making inquiries of the patient, soon learned about the girl and her grandmother. The doctor paid a visit to the grandmother, who said, "Well, I know nothing about the matter and I am no kahuna—as you know. But I think that if the man would promise to take the next ship for America and never return or even write back, he might recover."

The doctor tried to explain the situation to the still-unbelieving Irishman. Although he resisted at first, finally the patient was persuaded to take the grandmother's advice. The same day he was able to walk again, and that evening he caught a Japanese ship headed for the West Coast of the United States

How do the kahunas themselves see this whole process? Kahana, a Hawaiian *ana'ana* priest (priest of the dark forces), explained in an interview: "You are releasing the spirit from this encasement so it can go and get cleansed and purified and come back. It's time to take it out."

Long's story raises an issue that has often been disputed: does the victim have to believe in these powers in order to be susceptible to them? Dossey cites one researcher who contends that in such cases, "the victim, family members, and all acquaintances must accept the ability and power of the hexer to induce death. This belief must be commonly held with no exceptions."

Long's story contradicts this claim. The victim did not believe in such things and continued to scoff at them even as he was dying; moreover, nobody had even told him that the death prayer had been aimed at him. Attempting to write off such effects purely as a matter of suggestion would then be inaccurate (although it is easier for scientists to accept, since they feel obliged to dismiss actual occult causes from the outset). Indeed Michael Harner, the noted scholar of shamanism, observed that the Jivaro shamans of South America prefer the victim to be unaware of the psychic attack, because then he would take no measures to counter it. "Distant hexing is a security measure," he told Dossey in conversation.

Working with spirits is one time-honored way to cause harm; another way is closely related to it. This second approach involves sending not spirits but thought forms—mental images infused with vital energy that can thus make their effects felt in the physical world. The difference between the two methods is in the tools: a spirit is usually regarded as a living, more or less conscious entity, whereas a thought form is the creation of a human mind and has no independent existence.

Admittedly, the line between these two types of magic can be a thin and wavering one. In his *Meditations on the Tarot*, a contemporary classic of Christian esotericism, Valentin Tomberg writes that this method of creating a thought form is precisely how you create a demon.

> As with all generation, that of demons is the result of the cooperation of the male principle and the female principle, i.e., the *will* and the imagination, in the case of generation through the psychic life of an individual. A desire that is perverse or contrary to nature, followed by the corresponding imagina-

tion, together constitute the act of generation of a demon.

A term used in the occult literature for such entities is "egregore." One famous instance of the creation of an egregore is related by Alexandra David-Neel, a Frenchwoman of the early twentieth century who penetrated the then-forbidden country of Tibet to learn its occult practices. By dint of intense meditation, she was able to generate the form of a monk that took on a quasi-autonomous existence and even made its presence felt to other people. When the entity started to make a nuisance of itself, David-Neel had to devote another several months of intense meditation to destroying it.

Harming by means of thought forms does not necessarily require the generation of quasi-autonomous psychic entities. Dossey mentions the case of a patient of his, a woman afflicted with chronic fatigue syndrome. The woman was domineering and manipulative while her husband was extremely unassertive. He had always resented his wife; after she fell ill, he started to hate her.

One night, after a bitter argument, the husband stormed out of the house; when he returned, he found his wife dead. The man was overcome with guilt, convinced that his hatred had killed his wife. He refused to enter psychotherapy and instead joined an extremely conservative fundamentalist church, where he was able to assuage his conscience by believing that her death was the will of a wrathful God.

Psychologists sometimes employ the term "magical thinking." This involves the belief that an inner wish or emotion somehow caused an effect that later happened in reality. A four-year-old child, for example, may hate his brother and wish he were dead. The brother then dies; the child then believes that somehow he was the cause of the death. It is a version of the old logical fallacy *Post hoc, ergo propter hoc*: "After this, therefore *because of* this."

Clearly not every case of misfortune can be traced to someone else's negative thoughts, even if that person really did have those thoughts. Nor is it absolutely clear what the determining factor might be, but it very likely includes the intensity of the desire. A passing irritation that leads a person to say, "I wish he were dead!" probably does not have much effect in most cases. But when the thought is fed and nurtured with intense emotional energy, even unintentionally, it can begin to gain power. The man who thought he had killed his wife had probably directed a huge amount of hatred at her.

I myself once had a curious experience in this regard. A number of years ago I lived next to neighbors who were causing me a great deal of disturbance with their noise.

I had spoken to them about it, but it did no good except to change the source of the noise: their rock band practicing in the garage was supplanted by dogs who got on their roof and barked obnoxiously at everything. I felt the negative energy accumulating in myself, and although I intended no harm to them—I merely wanted them to stop disturbing me—a strange thing happened one day. I put a letter in their mailbox asking them yet again to deal with these issues; it was the only time I ever did that. Then I drove to work as usual and was gone for the rest of the day, only getting back late in the evening. The next morning I noticed something strange: a tall tree that had been directly next to their mailbox was gone. Neighbors later told me that a truck had hit that tree that day, and it had to be taken down. There is, of course, no way that I could prove that my thoughts had this entirely unintended effect, but I had never put anything in their mailbox before and never did again. The coincidence was disturbing, and I had the uncanny feeling of being at war with these neighbors; moreover I began to feel an intense psychic charge around my house. A few months later, not wanting the situation to escalate any further, I solved the problem by moving away.

Thus thought forms, in order to have power, need not have energy directed consciously at them; they can receive this force even when it arises spontaneously and unintentionally. But like spirits, these thought forms do require some energy or vital force in order to operate.

Having briefly surveyed some powerful though unsavory occult practices, what practical lessons can we draw? In the first place, wishing for harm to someone else is remarkably common; one poll indicated that 5 percent of Americans surveyed had done it (and we have to assume that this is a low figure, since it only accounts for those who were willing to admit as much). In the second place, it is remarkably dangerous. Indeed magical practices of any kind are dangerous, even when one's intention is reasonably pure; almost invariably something goes awry, producing results that are not exactly what you might have wanted. Occult magic is rather like trying to sculpt something out of nitroglycerin—a sloppy but also highly explosive material.

The problem is compounded when one is working with an intent to harm. It is extremely difficult, perhaps impossible, to create a thought form or invoke a spirit and remain totally disconnected from it. Thus if you are creating something negative, you can be sure that it will return to you in some form or another, just as in *huna* the spirits return to the kahuna after they have consumed a victim's energy. And they are not always easy to control when they are aroused, even by their supposed master.

To illustrate this point, Max Freedom Long tells another story, which happened to his mentor and informant about *huna*, an American scientist named William Tufts Brigham. During a trip to the Mauna Loa volcano to collect native plants, Brigham found that one of his servants, a twenty-year-old boy, started to fall ill. Although there was ostensibly nothing wrong with him, he began to waste away and, like the Irishman, lost feeling in his legs. The boy believed that he was being prayed to death, and Brigham's servants, who regarded him as a great kahuna, begged him to send the spirits back to the one who had launched them. "This is perhaps the easiest thing an amateur magician could be called upon to do," said Brigham. "The spell had been initiated and the trained spirits sent out. All I had to do was to put up the usual big arguments to talk the brainless things over to my side. . . . I stood over the boy and began to advance arguments to the spirits. I was smoother than a politician. I praised them and told them what fine fellows they were. . . . Little by little I worked around to tell them how sad it was that they had been made slaves by a kahuna instead of being allowed to go on to the beautiful heaven that awaited." Finally, mustering a supreme concentration of power and will, Brigham let out a tremendous roar. Soon the suffering boy felt better, and in an hour he was up and eating. Later

Brigham learned that the kahuna who had sent the curse had neglected to cover himself with the usual occult protection, and by the next morning he was dead.

Much the same is true with thought forms of the more impersonal variety. To begin with, the thought form, in order to have any effect upon the recipient, must find some resonance in him or her. The Theosophists Annie Besant and C. W. Leadbeater write: "In cases in which good or evil thoughts are projected at individuals, those thoughts, if they are to fulfill directly their mission, must find, in the aura of the object to whom they are sent, materials capable of responding sympathetically to their vibrations." Otherwise the thought form will bounce off.

> That is why it is said that a pure heart and mind are the best protectors against inimical assaults. . . . If an evil thought, projected with malefic intent, strikes such a body, it can only rebound from it, and it is flung back with all its own energy; it then flies backward along the magnetic line of least resistance, that which it has just traversed, and strikes its projector; he . . . suffers the destructive effects he had intended to cause to another.

These observations go far toward answering the final and perhaps most pressing question connected with toxic prayer: how do you protect yourself against it? A positive mindset is a good start, so purging thoughts of hatred, judgment, and violence from your mind is a necessity. It's also helpful to clear away negative thoughts that are aimed at yourself: recognize that thoughts of your own weakness, inferiority, vulnerability, and sickness are poisons and rid yourself of them. If this kind of thinking has been a lifetime habit, it may prove difficult to break, but even the smallest efforts can bring results and will also create a momentum that will gradually build.

For those with some ability at visualization, some of the standard forms of occult protection can be useful. The most common is probably envisaging yourself as surrounded by a sphere or ovoid form of white light. But the exact technique you use is probably less important than the clarity and power you bring to the thought, so you will probably do best by experimenting with which methods work for you. Conventional prayers can also be employed, such as the Lord's Prayer, which includes the petition "deliver us from evil." Again, the specific form of the prayer is not as important as whether it arouses a powerful and positive emotional response in yourself.

But perhaps the chief thing to remember is not to fear. Fear is a negative emotion and will weaken you far more than it will strengthen you, and it is probably no coincidence that the cultures in which psychic attack is most common are those that are pervaded by fears of black magic. For this reason, a healthy, grounded, common-sense mindset may be the best protection of all.

## SOURCES

Anonymous [Valentin Tomberg]. *Meditations on the Tarot: A Journey into Christian Hermeticism.* Translated by Robert A. Powell. Warwick, N.Y.: Amity House, 1985.

Besant, Annie, and C. W. Leadbeater. *Thought-Forms.* Adyar, Madras, India: Theosophical Publishing House, 1978 [1901].

Crowley. Aleister. *Magick in Theory and Practice.* New York: Castle, n.d.

David-Neel, Alexandra. *Magic and Mystery in Tibet.* New York: Dover, 1971.

Dossey, Larry. *Be Careful What You Pray For . . . You Might Just Get It.* San Francisco: Harper San Francisco, 1997.

Hertel, S. E. *"Kahuna Ana'Ana:* The One Who Walks in Darkness." *Gnosis* 14 (Winter 1990), 30–33.

Homer. *The Odyssey.* Translated by Samuel Butler: http://classics.mit.edu/Homer/odyssey.html; accessed March 10, 2009.

# Sixteen

# THE DUAL NATURE
# OF REALITY

THOUGHT, TAKEN FAR ENOUGH IN any direction, leads to an ultimate question: what is reality? What do we experience as real, and why do we do so?

This issue has preoccupied philosophers for thousands of years. In the end, they seem to come up with two radically different answers, and these answers have in and of themselves shaped not only schools of philosophy, but entire civilizations.

The first perspective underlies most of Western thought. From this point of view, there is little doubt about what is real. It is what we can see and feel and touch—in short, *things*. And in fact if we leave the definition to etymology, the matter is settled. After all, the word "reality" is derived from the Latin *res*, which means "thing." If we accept this perspective, it is *things* that are real. This is generally how we use the term in ordinary language: the real is what is material. Only a fool buys invisible real estate.

The greatest champion of this perspective was the Greek philosopher Aristotle, who said that what underlies reality is substance.[1] It would be hard to overestimate Aristotle's influence not only on Western philosophy, but even on ordinary notions of reality. By this view, whatever does not have substance that we can see or feel has a dubious claim to reality. The room I see before me now exists; the room I saw last night in a dream does not.

All this seems so obvious that it may look uninteresting. Of course, we may be tempted to say with impatience, the world of sensory appearances is real. How could it *not* be? The most famous argument in favor of this view was stated by the British philosopher G. E. Moore, who claimed he could prove the existence of external reality: "How? By holding up my two hands, and saying, as I make a certain gesture with the right hand, 'Here is one hand,' and adding, as I make a certain gesture with the left, 'and here is another.'"[2]

In one sense, Moore was right. If I were to offer you an airtight logical argument that proved that the hand in

---

[1] *The Encyclopedia of Philosophy*, Paul Edwards, ed. (New York: Macmillan, 1967), 1:156.
[2] G. E. Moore, "Proof of an External World," 166; quoted on http://plato. stanford.edu/entries/moore/; accessed Nov. 26, 2006.

front of you does not exist, would you believe me? Probably not. The evidence of your own senses would trump any form of reasoning, no matter how impeccable. As Moore wrote, "Which is more certain—that I know that I am holding a pencil in my hand or that the principles of the skeptic are true?"[3]

And yet there is something troubling about this view, and it has bothered philosophers for about as long as there has been such a thing as philosophy. In the first place, our senses frequently deceive us. To use a metaphor common in Indian philosophy, I see a snake in front of me. But on closer inspection, I see that it is actually a rope. What kind of reality, then, did the snake have?

Such simple errors may be easy to correct, but who is to say that our cognitive misreading of the world does not go much deeper than that? Even the most rigorous materialist must admit that our senses perceive only a narrow bandwidth of reality. If we have devised scientific instruments—telescopes, microscopes, and so on—to expand our horizons somewhat, in all likelihood this only expands the scope of our view to a tiny degree.

There is yet another problem with the common-sense view of reality. In the West, it was first stated by the Greek philosopher Parmenides in the fifth century B.C. How can

---

[3] Quoted in *The Encyclopedia of Philosophy*, 3:378.

the world of substance—that is, of appearances—have any reality when it is constantly changing from one thing into another? As Parmenides wrote, "How could what *is* thereafter perish? and how could it come into being? For if it came into being, it is not, nor if it is going to be in the future."[4]

Parmenides' views were highly influential on later philosophers, including Plato. Building on Parmenides' argument, Plato contended that what was real (because it was unchanging and eternal) was the world of Ideas or Forms, archetypal patterns that exist in a higher, intellectual reality.[5]

Despite Plato's tremendous stature, Western philosophy as a whole has not adopted his stance. The West has generally been far more comfortable with the views of Plato's pupil Aristotle, which correspond much more closely to common sense. The philosophy of India, on the other hand, has tended to be more comfortable with views like Plato's. While most Indian schools of philosophy do not speak of anything that corresponds to the Forms, they do generally accept Plato's criterion: that only what is unchanging is real. (In all likelihood, this view was formulated in India before Plato's time.)

---

[4]G. S. Kirk and J. E. Raven, *The Presocratic Philosophers* (Cambridge: Cambridge University Press, 1957), 273.
[5]See, for example, Plato, *Phaedo*, 78c–e; *Republic*, 508e–509a; 596b ff.

Hence we are left with two radically different criteria of reality: what we can see and feel and touch on the one hand, and what is eternal and unchanging on the other. It often seems that when philosophers dispute about this question, they are judging from different premises without realizing it.

Is there some way of reconciling the two? I believe there is, and it appears in the esoteric teachings of many traditions. To begin to understand it, let's return to the notion that what is ultimately real is the world of sensation. We already saw one problem with this point of view: it's hard to distinguish what is actually going on. Our minds and our senses deceive us. The snake may be a rope; the mouse I see in a room at twilight may be nothing more than a crumpled piece of tissue that missed the wastebasket. And then there are dreams, illusions, hallucinations—what about these?

Nonetheless, even if I am experiencing an illusion, I am still experiencing *something*. In this sense we may speak of one dimension of reality as *that which is experienced*. This view cuts through all the difficulties about the veracity of what I experience, whether it looks that way to others, and so on. To give this dimension of experience a traditional name, we can call it the *world*. (Of course this is not the world in the conventional sense of the planet Earth; it is the sum total of what we experience.)

If we grant that there is a reality that is experienced, we can see that it has certain characteristics. For one thing, it is eternally changing. Things mutate into other things; there is decay, death, destruction on the one hand; birth, creation, generation on the other. Even thoughts and dreams have life spans, following some mysterious cycles of their own. All of these make up the world. Viewed in this way, the world seems to be eternal, even if the individual things that appear to make it up are not. It goes on endlessly, and to all appearances it will continue to do so.

But this leaves another issue open. If we grant that there is something that is experienced, what is doing the experiencing? This is harder to pinpoint. It leads us to the question of subjective experience, another issue that has vexed philosophers for thousands of years, just as it is now perplexing psychologists and cognitive scientists. There has been endless debate about the "mind-body problem," for example, about whether our subjective experience is nothing more than the firings of some neurons—or if it is not, what else it might be.

Again, however, no matter what the ultimate cause of this experience may be, it remains true that there is something that *is experiencing*. It is that in us which says "I." But this is not the ordinary ego, with its thoughts and desires and judgments. Why? Because we can step back and look at all these things within ourselves. If we can look even at internal events, what is doing the looking? It would seem that the ego is merely a kind of anteroom to a larger, higher "I" that sits at the background of all our experience, watching it through our minds and bodies as through a telescope.

Moreover, this "I," whatever it is, also seems to be eternal—at least in the context of our individual lives. Whatever I experience, good or bad or indifferent, it always remains true that there is an "I" that is doing the experiencing.

Contemporary philosophy has grown skeptical about this "I." After all, one cannot cut up a body and find this "I" somewhere inside. Nor can one detect it in the endlessly complex series of neural processes that fascinate contemporary investigators. But in a sense one does not need to find it, because it is always there. It can never be seen, because it is always *that which sees*.

All this seems to come down to a fundamental polarity: between that which *experiences*, the "I," and that which is *experienced*, the "world." But then what about others? Am I the only sentient being in the world? If not, how do I know this? If we do not deal with this point, we are left with solipsism, the idea that we can ultimately know nothing apart from ourselves.

Here is where esoteric philosophy comes in. It tells us that ultimately this "I" is the same in all of us. While this may seem to make our view of the world not only bend but snap, it is the only conclusion that remains. And in any case, we pay lip service to it all the time. How many times have we said or heard, "We are all one"? What would this mean otherwise, what *could* this mean, unless it is simply an empty cliché?

This assertion that this "I" is ultimately one in all of us takes us fairly far from ordinary experience, but it is a truth that has been stated by sages and masters over and over. If it cannot be verified from the street-level point of view, it can be verified by certain spiritual practices— notably meditation in all its forms.

As I've said, these ideas appear in many different types of esoteric philosophy. In esoteric Christianity and Judaism, the "I" is sometimes called "I am." It is why, in the Kabbalistic tradition, "I am that I am" is the holiest of God's names, and it is also why the Gospel of John can have Jesus say, "I am the way, the truth, and the life" (John 14:6). Viewed from this inner dimension, it is not the personage known as the historical Jesus, but rather "I am," that is "the way, the truth, and the life," the "door," the "true vine."

What the Western esoteric traditions often speak about in veiled or allusive terms, the traditions of India discuss openly. The *Mandukya Upanishad* says, "The Self is the lord of all; inhabitant of the hearts of all. He is the source of all;

creator and dissolver of beings. There is nothing He does not know."[6] And one master of Advaita Vedanta writes, "From the absolute viewpoint, the Self alone is true; it is felt within as the 'I' or pure consciousness and pervades the external world as creative God."[7] The most common name for this Self in the Indian tradition is *Atman*.

The Samkhya, perhaps the oldest of all Indian philosophical systems, points to similar insights. What in this article I have called the "I," the Samkhya calls *purusha*; what I have called the "world," the Samkhya calls *prakriti*. Suffering arises when *purusha* identifies with *prakriti*, or, as we might say, when the "I" confounds itself with the world. The spiritual path, which is for a long time a process of detachment, is a means of gradually separating the "I" from the world, that is, separating consciousness from the contents of its own experience. At this point, supreme illumination takes place. The old world falls away, and a new one arises. Such is enlightenment.

The perspective set forth above may sound dualistic: that is, it may seem to isolate everything into two radically distinct forces that ultimately have nothing to do with each other. And it is true that the Samkhya, for example, is

---

[6]*The Ten Principal Upanishads*, trans. W. B. Yeats and Shree Purohit Swami (New York: Macmillan, 1937), 60.

[7]Kshitish Chandra Chakravarti, *Vision of Reality* (Calcutta: Firma K. L. Mukhopadhyay, 1969), 166.

usually characterized as a dualistic philosophy. Many people today speak of dualism contemptuously, yet without quite knowing why it deserves such treatment, much as people used to have a superstitious aversion to two-dollar bills. But dualism is not so easily discarded. It does seem to be true that this separation of the "I" from the world is only a stage in a lengthy process, and that in the end the essential unity underlying all things will be recognized. But dualism, if it is not a final stage, is a necessary one, much as the old alchemists had to perform *separatio* or separation on the matter they worked with before they could raise it to a higher unity. In short, there may well be a stage at which one realizes that "the nature of phenomena is nondual," as we read in a text of the Dzogchen school of Tibetan Buddhism.[8] But we may need to pass through the phase of duality before we reach it.

Is this process of detachment and reintegration ever complete? Will we ever be able to separate ourselves from a confused perception of reality so that we may return to the world in a new and more integrated form? The evidence of innumerable masters and mystical texts suggests that it is. I must immediately add, however, that I have never myself met anyone who seemed to attain this level

---

[8]Chögyal Namkhai Norbu, *Dzogchen: The Self-Perfected State*, trans. John Shane (Ithaca, N.Y.: Snow Lion, 1996; reprint), 81.

of full realization, which is sometimes called *enlightenment*. As a result, I cannot answer another question that seems to arise: is this realization of the Self, the recognition of one's absolute identity with the true Knower, itself a final goal? Or is it too merely another portal to dimensions of reality that are as far above it as enlightenment is above ordinary consciousness? Personally, I incline toward the latter view. And this would mean that both consciousness and the universe are multivalent, open-ended, and open to endless exploration. There is nowhere to stop, and there is always further to go.

### SOURCES

Larson, Gerald J. *Classical Samkhya*. 2nd ed. Delhi: Motilal Banarsidass, 1979.

# PUBLICATION CREDITS

"An Encounter with the Ancient Wisdom" originally published in *New Dawn*, May–June 2012

"Does Prophecy Work?" originally published in *New Dawn*, January–February 2007

"Secrets of *The Da Vinci Code*" originally published in *New Dawn*, Special Issue No. 2, 2006

"2012" originally published in *New Dawn*, January–February 2008

"René Guénon and the Kali Yuga" originally published in *New Dawn*, September–October 2010

"Atlantis Then and Now" originally published in *New Dawn*, March–April 2011

"Masonic Civilization" originally published in *Gnosis*, No. 44, summer 1997

"*A Course in Miracles* Revisited" originally published in *Parabola*, spring 2005

"Hidden Masters" originally published in *New Dawn*, March–April 2008

"Cultivating the Field of Images" originally published in *Parabola*, February 2001

"The Science of Thought" originally published in *New Dawn*, January–February 2011

"The Mysterious *Kybalion*" originally published in *New Dawn*, January–February 2011

"Demons Among Us" originally published in *New Dawn*, September–October 2009

"Toxic Prayer" originally published in *New Dawn*, May–June 2009

"The Dual Nature of Reality" originally published in *Quest: Journal of the Theosophical Society in America*, March–April 2007

# INDEX

# ABOUT THE AUTHOR

RICHARD SMOLEY has over thirty-five years' experience of studying and practicing esoteric spirituality. Educated at Harvard and Oxford Universities, he is the author of *Inner Christianity: A Guide to the Esoteric Tradition; Conscious Love: Insights from Mystical Christianity; The Essential Nostradamus; Forbidden Faith: The Secret History of Gnosticism; The Dice Game of Shiva: How Consciousness Creates the Universe; and Hidden Wisdom: A Guide to the Western Inner Traditions* (with Jay Kinney). Smoley is also the former editor of *Gnosis: A Journal of the Western Inner Traditions.* Currently he is editor of *Quest: Journal of the Theosophical Society in America* and of Quest Books.